SIX GATES OF HELL

JUGADU FAUJI

BLUEROSE PUBLISHERS
India | U.K.

Copyright © Jugadu Fauji 2023

All rights reserved by author. No part of this publication may be reproduced, stored in a retrieval system or transmitted in any form or by any means, electronic, mechanical, photocopying, recording or otherwise, without the prior permission of the author. Although every precaution has been taken to verify the accuracy of the information contained herein, the publisher assumes no responsibility for any errors or omissions. No liability is assumed for damages that may result from the use of information contained within.

BlueRose Publishers takes no responsibility for any damages, losses, or liabilities that may arise from the use or misuse of the information, products, or services provided in this publication.

For permissions requests or inquiries regarding this publication, please contact:

BLUEROSE PUBLISHERS
www.BlueRoseONE.com
info@bluerosepublishers.com
+91 8882 898 898
+4407342408967

ISBN: 978-93-93386-66-3

Cover Designer Instagram: **whats.up.momo**
Typesetting: Pooja Sharma

First Edition: August 2023

SIX GATES OF HELL

"Are you ready to undertake the challenging journey of a teenage boy through the rigorous National Defence Academy?"

Jugadu Fauji

Dedicated to

This book is dedicated to all my brother officers of the past, present, and future, as well as to all the aspiring members of the armed forces who will be the future leaders of this great country. So, "DO YOU HAVE IT IN YOU?"

Acknowledgments

Being a cadet at NDA, you are taught not to say "Sorry" or "Thank you." However, the army teaches you to be grateful and gracious. Therefore, I would like to express my gratitude to my seniors and juniors who motivated me to put my thoughts into writing.

This would not have been possible without my Instagram and YouTube families, who have always supported me and pushed me to greater heights.

"You can take a cadet out of NDA, but you can never take NDA out of a cadet."

Must Know

What Is NDA?

NDA, which stands for the National Defence Academy, is an iconic and prestigious institution located in Khadakwasla, Pune, Maharashtra. It is the world's first tri-services academy, meaning that cadets from all three services - the Army, Navy, and Air Force - train together before proceeding to their respective pre-commissioning academies for the grueling fourth year of training. NDA is more than just an academy; it is a feeling that cannot be described in words. It has produced the highest number of service chiefs of staff and numerous gallantry award winners.

Additionally, many cadets join the National Defence Academy twice a year, to be precise. As a result, the concept of battalions and squadrons has evolved to keep things manageable. On the reporting day, cadets are assigned to one of the 18 squadrons and 5 battalions. Each battalion and squadron has a rich history and unique traditions that the cadets follow with great reverence.

NO 1 Battalion - TIGER Battalion (ABCD)

- Alpha
- Bravo
- Charlie
- Delta

NO 2 Battalion - DOLPHIN Battalion (EFGH)

- Echo Squadron
- Foxtrot Squadron
- Golf Squadron
- Hunter Squadron

No. 3 Battalion - EAGLE Battalion (IJKL)

- India Squadron
- Juliet Squadron
- Kilo Squadron
- Lima Squadron

No. 4 Battalion - ABHIMANYU Battalion (MNOP)

- Mike Squadron
- November Squadron
- Oscar Squadron
- Panther Squadron

No. 5 Battalion - HAWKS Battalion (QR)

- Quebec Squadron
- Romeo Squadron

Each squadron at NDA comprises approximately 100 to 125 cadets and 125 rooms. Every squadron has its own customs and traditions and is represented by two unique colors. Cadets from various parts of India and friendly foreign countries are present here. This is a place where bonds are formed among the cadets and between them and their squadrons, ultimately leading to strong bonds with this great country over the years.

There is a saying at NDA:

"If you can't fight for two colors(referring to squadron), you will never be able to fight for three colors (referring to the Indian flag)."

NDA motto: "Service Before Self."

Contents

Gate 1: Dopes Are Born

Dream Do Come True 9

Yeah - I Got My Overstudy.. But He's A Total Jerk 18

Academy Waterloo 26

What Goes Around- Comes Around 34

NDA Special - The Wagon Of Dreams 42

Gate 2: The Mysteries

Cross Country - The Pandemonium 49

Camp Greenhorn 57

Liberty And Hockey!! 65

Novices Boxing & The Academics Torch 72

Gate 3: The Pillars

Being A Dad Isnt Easy! 81

The Responsibility! 86

A Cadet's Curse - The Rejection! 91

Gate 4: The Joshbox!

The Breaking Point 97

Rovers 102

Drill Competition 108

Gate 5: Rise Of The Kings!

    The Taste Of Power! 115

    A Birthday, A Broken Nose And A Feud! 122

Gate 6: Reign Of The Lords!

    My NDA Ball! 131

    My NDA POP! 138

    Epilogue 144

    Mission 100 146

Introduction

IIT, SCHOOL BOARDS OR NDA - A DILEMMA

"What will happen if I have to take a year off? My family's financial situation is poor, and the stress of studying is starting to affect my health. Please guide me through this difficult time, God."

It was January 25th when I received my call letter for SSB. For those who don't know about SSB, let me shed some light on it. The Services Selection Board, or SSB, is an organization that assesses candidates for becoming officers in the Indian Armed Forces. It is followed by a difficult written exam, and to add some spice, the selection rate of this organization is less than 1% (approximately 0.0015 including the written exam). So the journey was not going to be easy.

With the call letter in hand, I was fighting two emotions. I was thrilled that I could clear the written exam, but I was worried too, as the game had just begun! It was when I was struggling with my school preboards, mock tests for the IIT, and preparation for the SSB.

Having no idea about SSB, I was wasting hours and hours of my busy life on YouTube, and let me tell you, it was when you used to pay for data in GBs, unlike today, where 4G and 5G are available at very reasonable prices. So finally, somehow, I got my hands on a skinny and cheap book named "SSB: The Complete Guide" by KN Natrajan. Let me be very straight here - I am not promoting any book for SSB. I selected this book because it was the thinnest and cheapest on the market.

Only God knows how I managed to pass preboards at school, but deep down, I was happy that the book was in its last pages. Having no clear knowledge about SSB and putting all my faith in this sole book, finally, the day arrived when I was packing my bag for Allahabad. I still remember the night prior to SSB, when my dad sat next to me and said,

"Don't be so stressed out, son. It's just an interview. There is nothing in this world you can't achieve if you set your eyes on it. And even if you fail, you can always go for IIT or many other top universities, which you will be able to crack without breaking a sweat."

My dad, like any middle-class Indian dad, was worried about my future. He didn't have any degrees or PhDs, but I could clearly see in his eyes that he loved me more than anything. He was a typical example of a man who had worked hard throughout his life to build something for his family but had failed. However, failures had not diminished the fire that still burned brightly in his heart. He was still a dreamer and had aged like fine wine. He not only had complete faith in my capabilities but was also well-versed in my limitations. On the other hand, I had always been a bright child, a typical example of a child who had been in the top three throughout his life. But preparing for IIT had already made me realize that staying in the top three in school can't guarantee success because there are lakhs of schools in India and lakhs of toppers from the same schools.

His words were like a warm embrace, and I couldn't help but cry. Like most typical Indian sons, I didn't express my love for him before heading off to bed. As I lay there, my mind raced with worry.

"What will happen if I have to take a year off? My family's financial situation is poor, and the stress of studying is starting to affect my health. Please guide me through this difficult time, God."

The next morning, my dad woke me up in a hurry. We were running late for the train to Allahabad, and there was only an hour left before it departed. I quickly got ready, hugged my mother, said my morning prayers, and headed to the railway station with my dad. We made it to the train just in time, and with my mother and father by my side, I felt ready to face whatever came my way at "The Rejection Center—SSB Allahabad."

The next day, I had to report to the railway station at 1300 H, or 1 pm. I apologize for the military time format; it's what I'm used to. Dressed in a light blue shirt, dark blue trousers, and a tie I learned to wear from YouTube the night before, I stood on platform no. 1 with my dad at 1000 H. My dad was adamant about one thing in the military: punctuality. So, I stood there like a fool, three hours early.

As the reporting time drew nearer, I grew more and more anxious. My dad was just as nervous as I was, but he stood by my side with a proud and confident smile that spoke volumes: "This is my son, and he made it here on his own."

At 1230 H, the platform was crowded with many other young men who looked just like me - same shirt, trousers and tie. I double-checked my documents and said goodbye to my dad. He hugged me and said, "If you can't make it, the army doesn't deserve you."

With a wide grin on my face, I embraced my dad tightly and joined the line of candidates who had already arrived. It was my first time venturing out of my small village, and I soon realized that the world was full of different types of people: optimists, pessimists, friendly people, jealous individuals, and those who were rude for no apparent reason. I still recall one candidate who ridiculed me when I showed him the book I was studying for the SSB. His words stung as he laughed and said,

" You won't be selected. Officer-like qualities exist, and I can tell you don't possess any; this is my fifth SSB interview, and I have a better chance than people like you."

When I retorted, "Brother, this is my first attempt, and there won't be a second, I can't keep wasting my time and energy. I wish you the best of luck for your 5th, 6th, and 7th SSB," he grew flustered and infuriated. Despite this interaction, being an extrovert, I quickly made friends with others.

Soon enough, we boarded the army bus like goats being transported to the slaughterhouse. The bus stopped, and we arrived at our destination, SSB Allahabad. I was taken aback by the cleanliness and the high standards of discipline. One hoarding read, **"Do you have it in you?"**

After verifying our documents, we were assigned chest numbers and sent to our rooms. My chest number was 13, and I was concerned that it was unlucky. However, I discovered that tests were conducted in batches of 15-20 candidates, so I went to each candidate and offered some fruits and chips as a bribe to bring all 20 of us together. We chatted for 15 to 20 minutes, and we decided to give our best and support one another.

"Please don't create a fish market tomorrow. Everyone will have the chance to speak and express themselves. Let's act like gentlemen and crack this silly SSB," said chest number 17— Vikram, a smart and confident boy.

To everyone's surprise, over 60% of our small group survived after day 1. I underwent various tests in the following days, culminating in the interview. The story of what transpired during those five days is a tale for another day, available on my YouTube channel and Spotify. However, I recall one question from my interview: "What will happen if we don't select you?"

Reflecting on what my dad had told me at the railway station, I politely replied, "Sir, with all due respect, it will be a loss for the organization."

SSB was an adventure, and I managed to crack it, as my dad had predicted. After completing our medical examinations and receiving a clear ticket to the NDA, I packed my bag and left SSB Allahabad, where a man awaited me in the bright, hot sun. Drenched in sweat and with tears in his eyes, my dad hugged and squeezed me with all his might.

"See, I told you. There is nothing you can't achieve. " He tried to repeat himself, but his tears drowned out his words. He clung to me, weeping like a baby. Seeing my father cry, I burst into tears. We wiped each other's faces, booked a taxi to the railway station, and boarded the next train.

Sitting on platform number 1, I saw the hoarding that read, "Do you have it in you?" Fueled by a rush of excitement and energy, I shouted aloud, **"YES, I HAVE IT IN ME"**

gate 1:
dopes are born

1

DREAM DO COME TRUE

"Start doing 1,000 pushups, you cunts. "You have the nerve to talk back to your seniors," barked the alpha male.

It wasn't long before even Sharma realized that he was facing certain death. Adrenaline and fear coursed through our bodies as we began to do pushups. We felt no pain; fear had taken over our minds. We did 100 pushups, and soon we were kissing the ground.

"Small village boy makes history by cracking UPSC in his first attempt," read the headline of my local newspaper.

Upon my return to my village, I was greeted with great fanfare. Those who had doubted my abilities and potential in the past hugged me and congratulated me, saying, "Beta, I always knew you would do great things in life. God bless you, son."

My parents were overjoyed at my success, and I was grateful to have such supportive parents. A few days later, I received my call letter for NDA and began preparing to leave for Pune. As I was about to book a train ticket, my father insisted that I book a flight instead so that we could spend more time together.

As we drove to the airport, I felt as though there were only 12 hours in a day, and that time was slipping away. At the airport, I was lost in my own thoughts when my mother's eyes caught my attention. My mother was a symbol of strength and perseverance. She had married my father at the age of 18 and had never known much of the outside world. By the time she began to understand it, I was born. Now, I was her entire world. My mother had always desired education and had stood up against the orthodox society to complete her higher studies and graduation. Even though my father had always supported her, she understood the importance of education in one's life. She had always wanted me to be educated and achieve the success that she had not. Tears streamed down her face as she looked at me, her eyes shining with pride.

I wiped her tears and promised her that I would be back soon. "They say it's a great city, and the academy is so big. I will call you once I settle down in NDA," I said.

My mother kissed my forehead and said, "Take care of yourself, son; focus on your training, and don't worry about us. I will write you letters and send you sweets." She couldn't finish her sentence and began to sob. I held her tightly, and it was then that my father said, "Beta, you have a flight to catch. Hurry up now."

I touched their feet and headed towards the flight counter. I remember requesting a window seat from the flight attendant, as it was my first time flying. The flight attendant was kind enough to grant my request.

When I landed in Pune, I was amazed by the beauty of this small city. It was clean, had large roads and highways, and was just perfect. I hired a taxi from the airport and headed towards NDA Khadakwasla. The taxi dropped me off at Pashan Gate, where my details and the driver's details were checked, and we were directed towards a building called NJ Nair Hall.

NJ Nair Hall, named after the highly decorated officer Colonel Neelankantan Jayachandran Nair, is one of the grandest structures I have ever seen. Senior cadet appointments and drill instructors stood outside as I approached the hall. I approached a drill instructor and asked,

"Uncle - kaha Jana hai uncle?"

(Uncle - Where do I have to go?)

The drill instructor was not pleased with my address and berated me,

"Uncleeeee...Uncle bolta hai theelaa thala motaaa cadet (*How dare you call me uncle - You fat and lazy cadet*)?"

He pointed me towards the entry gate of NJ Nair Hall. Realizing my mistake, I addressed everyone as "sir" and quickly made my way towards the gate. Outside the hall, another drill instructor checked my documents and allowed me to enter. I was in awe as I stepped into the fully air-conditioned hall, which reflected discipline and decorum. All the chairs were blue, with an embossed NDA insignia on them, and all the cadets who had reported before me were sitting in silence. A stage in the center of the hall had two tables, one labelled Adjutant and the other Assistant Adjutant. I was asked to sit in the front row with my coursemates, who were being called to the stage one by one by the Adjutant.

The Adjutant was a tall, handsome army officer in uniform, someone I aspired to become one day. His stare sent shivers down my spine as he looked up from writing. I was hungry and thirsty, but his stare shook me to the core, and all I felt was fear. To my right, another coursemate named Sharma joined me, and he shouted,

"Aur bhai- kha se hai londey?"

(*Brother, where are you from?*)

Before I could respond, the cadet sitting on my left gave us a cold stare, and I knew death was inevitable in this academy. This cadet was Harry, a tall, bright, and athletic boy who would become my Senior Cadet Captain in the next three years. He was from a training school called RMS and was well-versed in the discipline part of the NDA.

Soon it was my turn to go to the stage, and I trembled with fear as I sat in front of the Adjutant.

"Do you play games?" he asked politely, and I knew it was the silence before the storm.

"Sir, I play carrom, chess, cricket, and KHO-KHO," I said with confidence.

The Assistant Adjutant laughed and mocked me,

"Bhai koi team game khelta hai kya.. KHO KHO.. KHO KHO. Bwahahaha yha kya KHO KHO khelne aaya hai??"

("*Brother, do you play any team game? And KHO KHO.. KHO KHO.. Bwhahahahah.. Have you come here to play KHO KHO in this academy?*").

In a low voice, like a chicken about to be culled, I said, "Sir, I play hockey and football." The Adjutant wrote something on a slip of paper and handed it to me. The slip read:

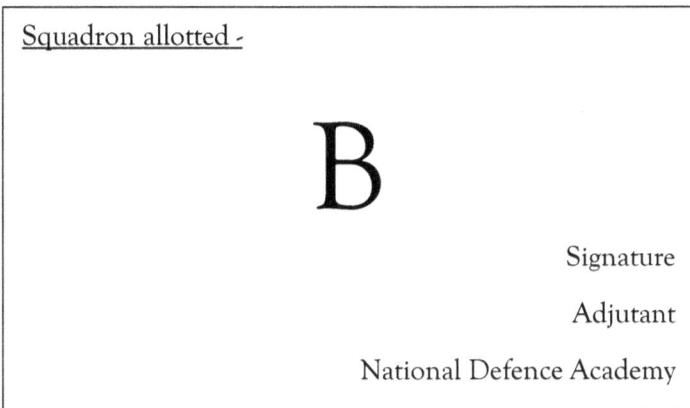

I struggled to read the slip, trying to make sense of the word 'Squadron' even though I had it upside down. Before I could process everything, I blurted out, "What is this 'B' thing?"

The adjutant responded with great courtesy, "This will be your home from today onwards. This is the place where you will transform from a boy to a man."

Confused, I began to ask, "Sir, but what-" but was abruptly interrupted by the assistant adjutant's barking. Only then did I realize just how kind and chivalrous the adjutant had been.

The moment I heard the assistant adjutant's harsh words, "Now get up and f*ck offfffff from here you specimen. You have too many doubts? Saab take him outside and solve all his questions," I felt offended. However, my relief grew as I realized that at least someone had been instructed to help me with my queries.

Soon enough, a drill instructor with an impressive mustache arrived to solve my doubts. But before I could say anything, he commanded,

"Cadet lagao 10,000 pushup - Ready go shoot!"

(*The ignoramus drill instructor barked orders, urging me to start doing 10,000 pushups with great haste*)

As soon as the drill instructor commanded me to do 10,000 pushups, I felt a wave of panic wash over me.

"10,000!! 10,000 Saab mai mar jaunga.. mere se nhi hoga" (*10,000!! 10,000 saab I will surely die. I won't be able to do it*), I pleaded, hoping he would spare my life.

But his response was cold and heartless,

"Mar jana - par pehle 10,000 pushups karke ke marna. wese bhi tum jese bekar cadet ki zroorat nhi hai fauj ko. Pushups shuru kaarrrrrrr"

(*You surely can die - but complete 10,000 pushups first, as such there is no need of useless cadets like you in this army.. Starttttt doing pushups*), he yelled, his mustache twisting into a demonic snarl.

In a state of pure fear, I hit the ground and began doing pushups. I was soon joined by my fellow cadets Harry and Sharma, who were also alloted the B squadron. We pushed ourselves to the limit, doing pushups until our arms went numb, our pristine uniforms turned to dirt, and we were reduced to dry-humping the ground due to the lack of strength in our arms.

Despite the pain and suffering, we pushed through, determined to succeed in this gruelling training and prove our worth as cadets.

The drill instructor sneered at us,

"Mai yaha aane se pehle OTA Chennai mai tha, wha par LC (Lady cadet) rehti hai aur wo bhi tum jese nakaraa cadets se behtar haii"

(*I was in OTA Chennai before coming here in NDA. There are lady cadets there. And you know what even they are better than pathetic losers like you*).

As we struggled to our feet, we were greeted by a sergeant from our squadron. In NDA, a sergeant is a fifth-term appointment, and this guy seemed harmless enough - until he started barking orders at us.

"Double up, you ladies. What's with those soft feet? Can't you run, haaan?" He shouted, pedalling his bicycle alongside us.

Sharma hissed under his breath,

"Khud saala cycle pe hai aur hume bol rha bhagne ko"

(*This moron is commanding us to run while he is himself on his cycle*).

"What did you say? What did you say, huh? Oh, so you're one of those brave ones, those who show their courage for the first ten minutes and then beg for mercy on their knees! I will turn you into a specimen," barked the sergeant.

"Sir...it's nothing like that. I just wanted to ask where I can get a bike like yours," said Sharma.

"Oh, you'll get it soon. Now start running, you ladies," shouted the sergeant.

We were drenched in sweat and gasping for air as we approached a tall building. It was nearly night, and I was already half-dead. But the sight of the structure made my eyes light up in the darkness. And let me tell you, it wasn't just a building. It was a dream come true. It was as magnificent as Leonardo da Vinci's Mona Lisa, as unique as Shah Jahan's Taj Mahal, and as tall as Angel Falls in Venezuela. It was just perfect.

And just as I was taking in the magnificence of the squadron that would be my home for the next three years, I heard someone shout at us. "Why the hell are you standing, assholes? Hurry up and bend!" A man emerged from the shadows. He was a heavily built, six-foot-tall alpha male in his twenties. He was the hunter, and we were his prey. "What's wrong with your ears?" "I said, bend!" he bellowed. Before we could even process his words, our reflexes kicked in, and we were soon on our hands.

"Start doing 100 pushups!" he commanded.

"Abe dimag khrab ho gya hai kya? Socha tha room milega, gaadi milegi. Subh se har koi pushups hi karwa rha "

("Hey, what's the deal? I thought we'd be getting a room and a car. Everyone's been making us do pushups since morning!") exclaimed Sharma, unaware that a few more words could cost him his life.

"Start doing 1,000 pushups, you cunts." "You have the nerve to talk back to your seniors," barked the alpha male.

It wasn't long before even Sharma realized that he was facing certain death. Adrenaline and fear coursed through our bodies as we began to do pushups. We felt no pain; fear had taken over our minds. We did 100 pushups, and soon we were kissing the ground. For a moment, my body touched the earth, and in that very instant, I fell asleep. I was at home, eating parathas. The dream was shattered by a loud noise.

"Wake up, you weakling! Are you humping the ground? How dare you sleep on this sacred parade ground?" the man yelled. The man soon went for a run, leaving us in the care of the same sergeant. Even the sergeant had started to feel sorry for us. He showed us our cabins. I was assigned cabin number 79, which I didn't realize until the next morning.

I entered the cabin and, with all my energy, asked, "Who was that guy outside, sir?"

"He's our SCC – Senior Cadet Captain," replied the sergeant.

"SCC...Senior...Cad...Cap..." I trailed off, and before I knew it, I had dozed off. My arms no longer hurt, and I wasn't worried about taking a shower or changing my clothes. I was with my mom again, enjoying parathas. I was dead asleep.

2

Yeah - I Got My Overstudy.. But He's A Total Jerk

Overstudy: Overstudy is a third termer in academy who is one year senior to you and teaches you everything!

"Start creamrolling you ass*****." Said my overstudy.

"Thank you, sir, but I am full. I just had my lunch." I said this, thinking that creamrolling has something to do with the dish - cream-roll.

"Shhhh! Don't speak," said a boy inside my cabin. "Yes, sir!" I exclaimed loudly.

"Don't shout, you moron," scolded the same boy. "Sorry, sir," I replied in a low voice.

"Stop calling me sir - I am your coursemate," said the boy emerging from the shadows. "

I said "okay, sir." The word 'sir' was so ingrained in my brain that I used to address civilian sweepers and other workers as 'sir' for the initial two weeks.

Getting back to the story, the boy was Harshal Sati, and he was my coursemate. Then he whispered,

"Crossing chal rahi hai bahar bhai." (*"Crossing is going on outside, my brother,"* he explained).

"What is this crossing, brother?" I asked in a hushed tone.

"Whenever a senior is being punished, we juniors are not supposed to witness it. We should disappear from the scene," said Sati in a hushed tone.

"How do you know all of this?" I asked.

"I am from Sainik School Ghodaghal, and I know everything," replied Sati.

"Teach me, brother," I said.

"No, you are useless. Ask your overstudy," he said, his disgust palpable. With that, he left my room, disappearing down the corridor once it was clear.

I didn't have the energy to feel bad and fell asleep again within seconds. However, my slumber was abruptly interrupted by someone singing at the top of their lungs.

"Pay attention Bravo Squadronnnnnnnnn

Allllllllll first to third termerssss SPRINT DOWN to SALARIA LOBBYYYYYY. Immediately Immediately Immeditely.

Allllllllll first to third termerssss SPRINT DOWN to SALARIA LOBBYYYYYY. Immediately Immediately Immeditely.

For a fleeting moment, I thought it was some sort of song or announcement for our welcome party. But then, I heard the thundering of footsteps. The walls of our squadron shook as if a herd of elephants was stampeding through.

In the next moment, I heard a familiar voice banging on my door.

"Jaldi kar! Announcement ho gayi hai!" *(Hurry up! The announcement has been made!)*

It was Harshal Sati. When I saw his face, I was convinced that it wasn't a dream. He had actually been in my cabin last night!

"What announcement?" I asked, bewildered by the commotion that had already begun.

"Just come outside, and for God's sake, wear your pants!" Sati shouted.

I quickly got dressed and ran my fingers through my beautiful locks of hair. As I stepped outside my cabin, I was transported to a whole new world.

As I stepped out of my cabin, I was greeted by a maze of wooden doors with brass knobs on both sides. The interior was adorned with beautiful red tiles, and there were three different sets of stairs: one in the centre and two on either side. I was lost in the interior decoration of my squadron when my eyes fell on the Senior Cadet Captain (SCC) standing on the central staircase. I didn't know where to go until I saw Sati standing with a group of cadets, including Harry and Sharma.

But before I could even take a step forwards, a barrage of insults and commands came my way.

"You fucking IKKI - you want to walk!" shouted a fifth termer.

"Start rolling, you fucker!" shouted all the fourth termers.

"Start knee to chest. No, start 20 whiskeys, start 100 helicopters!" shouted all the third termers in unison.

"Silence!" bellowed the SCC. "You fucking dimwits, can't you see your pop is standing here? You - Ikki," he pointed at me, "hurry up and join up with your coursemates."

I quickly made my way towards my coursemates, relieved that the SCC had intervened. But the relief was short-lived. The third termers soon descended upon us, shouting and commanding us to become murga and murgi.

Amidst the chaos, I met a thin guy named Ashish, who offered some words of encouragement. "Don't worry, bhai; learn as much as you can in the next 14 days, and don't feel low or sad. Adjust as soon as possible, mingle with your coursemates. Even I was a first-termer once. Time does fly here, and before you know it, you'll be back home," he said.

But just as I was beginning to feel comfortable, another guy, who looked like a classic villain from a movie, shouted at me to start doing pushups.

"I am Chaudhary, and he is Ashish. We are your overstudies," he said.

"Two overstudies? Two! Oh God, why?" I muttered to myself as I began doing pushups.

Then I was told to get up and join my fellow coursemates to get our bikes issued.

ACADEMY GARLAND

As I looked at the 21 boys lined up before me, I couldn't help but feel a sense of excitement and anticipation. Our sergeant sat on his cycle, ready to lead us on our next mission.

"Start running, ladies. Today is the day you will be issued bikes," he barked, his voice echoing through the air. I vividly remember one of my coursemates asking,

"Sir, can I get a Harley Davidson? I don't like speed bikes."

With that, all 21 of us took off at full throttle for MT Park, eager to claim our bikes and proudly wear them like garlands back to our squadrons. But first, we had to endure the demonic barber shop, where the barber transformed us into Vin Diesel lookalikes—smart yet bald. After our haircuts, we received a crash course in NDA basics, including how to do a front and back roll. While rolling may have seemed like a punishment at first, it actually strengthened our backs and made us more agile.

I remember a humorous incident that occurred after my haircut.

"Start creamrolling, you ass*****," my overstudy said.

"Thank you, sir, but I'm full - I just had my lunch," I replied, thinking that creamrolling was some sort of dish.

In the days that followed, I quickly learned that "silence was the key" and that anything with a funny-sounding name was definitely a form of punishment. I adopted the silent mantra "Observe, Orient, Decide, and Act"—commonly known as the OODA loop in the military—to help me navigate the tough times ahead.

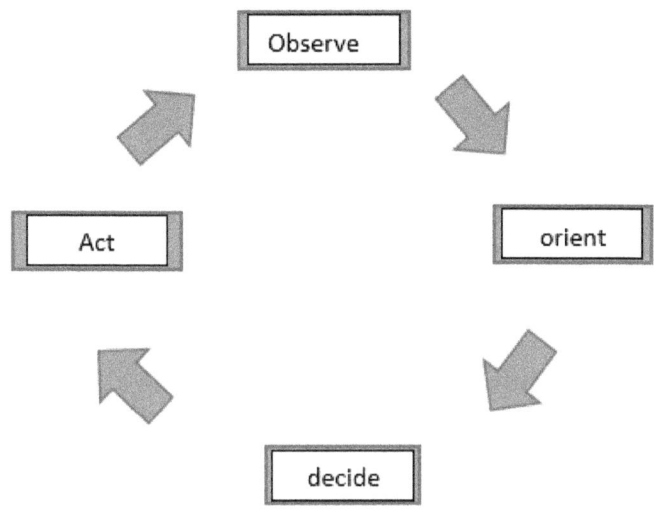

I was given the task of bringing tea for the seniors and sweeping the corridor every day. My two overstudies were great teachers, but they had completely different approaches. One was patient and used love as a means of instruction, while the other used punishments and was like a devil in human form. By the time my basic orientation was over, it was time for night PT, where we were forced to do multiple exercises, mostly pushups. And by the time night PT was over, it was almost midnight. I remember that after the first day was over, I couldn't even lift a jug to drink water. At 0030H, I set my alarm for 0400H , as instructed by my overstudy, and I laid down on my bed.

"Oh, my back feels so happy and relaxed," I thought to myself as I lay down on my bed. By the time I managed to remove my clothes, I was already fast asleep.

In NDA, every hour feels like an eternity, with every second spent battling through the pain. During the first few days, we were also taught the basics of NDA, which included a memorable visit to the washroom. I quickly realized why they say to "expect the unexpected" in NDA. To my surprise, there were no curtains or separate stalls—only a row of showers with naked cadets taking a bath. Feeling shy and unsure of what to do, I was promptly greeted by a fifth-termer who bellowed,

"So you're one of the new pussies who joined this time. Sorry, NDA doesn't have a separate bathroom for you to wash your twat. Hurry up and strip now."

Feeling embarrassed, I immediately stripped down and entered the shower. However, as soon as a drop of water hit my head, the fifth-termer barked again,

"You want to take your sweet time, huh? You have ten seconds to wash your cunt." I thought to myself, "Ten seconds? Is he insane?"

"Nine, eight, seven," he started counting down. I had barely managed to apply soap to my head when he said,

"Three, two, one. Your time is up. Now fuck off from here."

I tried to plead with him, "Sir, I have soap on me. Please let me wash it off."

"Listen, you piece of shit. You're new here, so I'll ignore your mistake this time. Don't open your mouth in front of your pops. Now, I don't care if you wipe it off or lick it off. Just fuck off from here."

I grabbed my towel and ran for my life, not knowing that in a few months, I'd be able to shower in just five seconds!

Another valuable lesson I learned was about mess etiquette and fine dining. I was in awe of the mess's beauty when I first entered. Everything was clean and orderly, with each squadron having its own set of tables. It looked like something out of a James Bond movie. But it was also the place where I had my first confrontation with my CSM (Cadet Sergeant Major), whom we affectionately referred to as the "Cadet Screwing Machine."

"So, you're a first termer," he said.

"Yes, sir. But who are you?" I asked, unaware that he was about to become a major thorn in my life.

"Close your plate," he said patiently.

"But, sir, I haven't finished eating yet," I protested.

"Close your fucking plate and get the fuck out of this mess!" he shouted at the top of his voice.

I was no longer hungry. I soon realized that I had made a grave mistake. I paid a heavy price that evening by enduring the "cream-rolling" punishment all night outside his cabin. The initial few days were full of learning and punishment. The only peaceful times were during classes, when we slept our hearts out, or when we were getting our stores issued. The new cadets were given a set of items, such as shoes and clothes, from Kapoor and Sons and the Quartermaster Fort. These were the places where we met other first-termers like ourselves from other squadrons and made new friends. We laughed and commiserated with each other about the trials and tribulations of NDA life. Everything outside the squadron was peaceful for us. We hardly knew at the time that we would be willing to die for the same squadron one day and would cherish its memories in a few years. But for now, it was a pain in the ass, and I wanted to get rid of it as soon as possible!

3

Academy Waterloo

"Why does everyone look so pale before jumping? It doesn't even seem that high," I exclaimed, unaware of the senior cadets surrounding me.

"You only realize the height of the 10-meter jump when you're standing on the board," replied a second-termer, his legs trembling slightly.

Every day at NDA was tough, without a doubt. If someone claims that NDA is easy, he is either lying or an ex-NDA. We were punished for almost everything. Most of my time was spent rolling or doing pushups, with the balance spent crying alone in dark corners. My pro tip for those who enter NDA: become friends with your coursemates as soon as possible. Your happiness will double, and your sorrow will be halved when someone you know is around to share both. Unfortunately, I had no such tip and spent most of my time alone, crying.

"Where the hell is my tea?" shouted Virender, the fifth termer next to my cabin.

"Sorry, sir, it was actually Ahmed's turn. I was supposed to broom today," I replied with tears in my eyes.

"Sorry? Sorrrrryyyyy? Who's your overstudy? And you, fucking runt, you want to put up your coursemate? Fuck off from here and go call your overstudy," said Virender mercilessly.

After a series of new and innovative punishments, I learned two lessons that day.

Lesson 1 - You should not say sorry or thank you to your seniors in the academy. If you make a mistake, you get punished. It is as simple as that.

Lesson 2 - YOU NEVER PUT UP YOUR COURSEMATE! This means you don't play the blame game with your coursemates.

The initial few days were very challenging. Getting up early in the morning and having sleepless nights made me think about quitting. But as they say, "Fire is the test of gold, adversity, of strong men." Every day, I motivated myself by saying, "DLTGH is 149 now; only 149 days, and I'll be home." For those who don't know, DLTGH stands for Days Left To Go Home, and DLTGH in the NDA is sacred. You might get punished for telling the wrong DLTGH. I still remember the day a senior made me roll for two hours for telling the wrong DLTGH. His words still echo in my ears.

"Piddly first termer. You don't know the DLTGH? You seem to be enjoying your life here. I will take all the fun out of you. Now start rolling, you...fuckinggg...ikkki."

The routine in NDA was like a monkey show. Every day started with getting ready for either PT or drill, sometimes even for both. It was followed by a crisp punishment session that made us late for breakfast, resulting in late attendance in classes, which in turn resulted in more punishment.

I remember missing breakfast almost every day, and doing all sorts of weird punishments—for poor mess etiquettes, for being late for classes, for not standing properly, and sometimes even for not breathing properly during swimming classes.

But punishments were the only thing that forged camaraderie between coursemates. I remember the day when I was crying in class for missing breakfast. A hand extended towards me to give me two biscuits of Parle-G.

"Hide it; keep your head down. If someone sees you eating in class, you will get more punishments. Don't look at me like that; that was my last reserve of stored rations," said Piyush, another coursemate who was my all-time saviour.

The days kept progressing, and we kept on getting punished. On the seventh day, we were told that we were having a "10-metre jump." I remember one afternoon when I returned from lunch, and my overstudies were waiting for me.

I was prepared for what was about to happen, having already come up with ten different punishments I knew I would endure in the next few minutes. However, to my surprise, they jumped on me and asked,

"Do you know how to swim?"

"No, sir, I don't," I replied.

"Listen, buddy, today is the 10-metre jump. It's nothing great, just 10 meters. Don't look down; don't think; just jump. The

Bravo Squadron cadets are known as the braves for a reason. Take a deep breath and jump," my good overstudy encouraged.

The evil overstudy intervened, "Listen, you piece of shit. If you don't jump, I will kill you. And your poor family, who thinks that you're training, will never get to know anything. I will bury you under the battalion dustbin, where you rightly belong. Understood?"

"Yes, sir," I said, now fully aware that it wasn't a joke. I looked around and saw all the overstudies motivating or threatening their understudies to jump. I realized that this was something important, and denying it would only reward me with a place in heaven. Soon, an announcement for the squadron fall-in was made, and all 120 boys stood in silence. From first to sixth termers, they were standing like dead bodies, as if they had seen a ghost. The door of the SCC's cabin opened, and out came our SCC already in sports rig.

"Listen, all of you cunts. Today is a big day for all of us. Today is the day where we start this term with confidence, positivity, and, of course, bravery. It's the first event of our squadron, and nobody must refuse. I repeat, nobody must refuse. I have kept 500 rupees on my study table, and if you dare to refuse, just reach the squadron before me, grab those 500 rupees, get a bus, and flee to your mother. Because I will chop you into pieces and throw you to the dogs. Understood?" SCC announced.

"Sir, yes, sir," shouted everyone in unison.

"Listen all of you! You have exactly 40 seconds to change into your sports rig and grab a towel. Move quickly and fall back in line in front of me!" bellowed SCC.

As a new cadet, I used to scoff at the seemingly impossible time limits set by our seniors. How could anyone possibly complete these tasks so quickly? But within a week, I found myself keeping pace with the others. I moved with lightning speed, climbing stairs as if I could fly, changing clothes while running, and multitasking like a pro. It was amazing to see what the human body is capable of. Even now, as I write this, I am astonished by the sheer determination and skill of an NDA cadet. If I were asked to climb three floors and change clothes in 40 seconds today, I would surely fail.

As the time ticked away, we all fell into line once again, ready to march to the swimming pool. Grabbing our bicycles, we set off on a mad dash to our destination. At the pool, we quickly showered and changed into our swimming trunks. The serene atmosphere was shattered as the jumping began. The sixth termers of Alpha Squadron went first, followed by their juniors. And soon it was our turn to climb the daunting 10-metre board. It was an incredible sight to behold.

Excitement and anticipation filled the air as our turn to climb the daunting 10-meter board approached. We watched in awe as the senior cadets of Alpha Squadron fearlessly leapt off the board, their bodies slicing through the water with grace and precision. As our turn drew near, a mix of nerves and adrenaline coursed through our veins. But we were determined to show what we were made of and prove our worth as NDA cadets.

"Why does everyone look so pale before jumping?" "It doesn't even seem that high," I exclaimed, unaware of the senior cadets surrounding me.

"You only realize the height of the 10-metre jump when you're standing on the board," replied a second termer, his legs trembling slightly.

Little did I know that the fear of the 10-metre jump was no joke. I've witnessed even the bravest cadets breaking down in tears and begging the ustaad to spare them from the event. The jumping board has a way of humbling even the most confident cadets, and I was about to experience it firsthand.

As our turn finally arrived, our SCC took to the board first. Rather than simply jumping, he flawlessly executed a handstand dive from a 10-metre height. Watching him, I felt an overwhelming sense of pride, knowing that our SCC wasn't a crybaby, but a true leader leading by example. The rest of our sixth termers followed suit, each jumping with confidence and shouting out their squadron's battle cry.

With their display of leadership, the atmosphere changed entirely. Those who had been trembling with fear now radiated energy, and those who had been hiding behind their coursemates were now eager to take the leap before their seniors. This, my friends, is what true leadership looks like.

When our SCC emerged from the pool, he asked who would be jumping first. Without hesitation, I raised my hand high in the air, my heart swelling with pride for my SCC. But when I turned around, I saw that all the first termers had raised their hands as well, their eyes gleaming with the hope that they too would one day become fine cadets like our SCC. This is leadership at its finest.

As I've been asked numerous times what defines leadership in one line, I'll answer it now:

Leadership is the ability to influence your team to take action willingly.

> **"Leadership is the art of getting someone else to do something you want done because he wants to do it".**
>
> **- General Dwight Eisenhower**

I vividly remember my first jump from the 10-metre board. My seniors had warned me not to look down, but curiosity got the better of me. I peeked over the edge, and the Olympic-sized pool seemed tiny. The distance from the board to the water felt like miles away. The thought of hitting the water at such a high speed terrified me, and I almost backed out. But the stern gaze of my ustaad made me think twice, and I took the leap of faith.

As I descended, I remembered the concept of acceleration due to gravity and braced myself for the impact. The water felt like a warm embrace at first, but soon enough, I found myself struggling to stay afloat. The ustaad yelled at me to use my hands, but I couldn't seem to keep my head above water.

Just as I was about to lose consciousness, someone pulled me up by the arm. It was the same ustaad who had given me the cold stare earlier. I coughed up water and tried to compose myself, but the overstudy had other plans. He berated me for being reckless and ordered me to change into a PT rig and report to him when I reached the squadron. I was disappointed by his lack of empathy and wished for some recognition for my bravery.

However, my attention quickly turned to another first termer who was crying on the diving board. The sight made me smile, and my SCC noticed.

"Get up there and motivate your coursemate," he commanded.

I climbed up the stairs once more and pleaded with Ahmad to jump. When he refused, our SCC took matters into his own hands and pushed him into the pool. After several attempts, Ahmad finally took the plunge, and we all celebrated his success.

In the end, Ahmad saved us from the evening PT, and we all looked up to him as our hero for that day. The experience taught me the true meaning of bravery and leadership: facing your fears and inspiring others to do the same.

4

What Goes Around- Comes Around

"Start doing 1000 pushups, Bammel sir!" I said it to my CSM with the utmost confidence.

"Brother, I never punished you this hard! Why are you seeking revenge?" replied Bammel sir.

"It's karma, sir. What goes around comes around. Now, get to it!" I reiterated.

After completing the daunting ten-meter jump, the entire squadron shifted its focus to other activities like cross country and games. As first-termers, our primary goal was to pass our PT and swimming tests on the first attempt. However, this was no easy feat, as we were put through rigorous exercises throughout the day. Our schedule was packed from morning ODT (outdoor training) to classes, lunch, post-lunch PT, study period, dinner, post-dinner PT, cabin PT, and finally, ODT again. With no time for recreation, I couldn't help but envy my seniors, who had passed their DST (Drill Square Test) and were allowed to venture into the city on Sundays. Meanwhile, sixth-termers wielded enormous powers and authority.

As a lowly first-termer, my dreams were modest. They ranged from getting enough sleep to making a girlfriend in Pune to visiting the gole market (a local market in NDA) on Sundays and being senior enough to indulge in evening snacks like cold coffee and pastries. Speaking of which, the cold coffee available in the NDA is heavenly and exclusive to the senior cadets.

Days passed by at a sluggish pace, but every morning, I reminded myself of the reason why I had embarked on this journey. This kept me going, even on the toughest days. Eventually, I passed my PT and swimming tests, making life a little easier. Passing on the first attempt earned me respect from my seniors, and I was treated better. Plus, I was ecstatic to be done with pushups and move on to more exciting exercises like chin-ups and toe touches. Although I recommend passing the tests on the first attempt, I urge you not to be discouraged if you can't. Dedication and consistency are what matter most. I know cadets who passed their PT on the last attempt and are excelling in all aspects of life.

For cadets, the midterm is a major motivator, marking the end of the first half of the term. Those who pass all their tests can take a short leave, making it a highly coveted milestone. Unfortunately, none of the first-termers, including myself, had passed the Drill Square Test and were ineligible for leave. However, our course had excelled in PT tests and novice cross-country, leading our squadron commander to gift us with the Panchmarhi Hike. Panchmadi, also known as Satpura ki Rani, is a hill station in the central Indian state of Madhya Pradesh. The five-day hike was one of the best experiences of my life, and it allowed us to bond with coursemates from other squadrons.

After midterm, my morale was at an all-time high, and even punishments seemed easier to bear. I remember being kept awake for seven days by my overstudy for a minor mistake of smiling in front of a senior during punishment. However, I smiled again after those seven sleepless nights, showing my mental toughness and fearlessness to my overstudy. This incident strengthened our bond and resulted in a conversation on the seventh night.

"Are you feeling sleepy? Do you want to rest?" he asked.

"No, sir," I replied, struggling to maintain my "murga" position on a small teapoy table.

"If you promise to leave your ego aside and stop smiling, I'll let you sleep. I'm tired of punishing you every night," he said.

"No, sir," I replied, standing in a puddle of sweat.

"Get up and sit here," he said, pointing to the chair in his study. It was the first time I sat in his cabin; usually, I either did pushups or cream-rolls in his cabin.

"Don't you feel sleepy? It's been seven days now," he asked.

"Yes, sir, I do feel sleepy," I replied, without any justification.

"You're the first asshole who smiles like a young whore all the time. This smile will get you fucked very hard someday," he said.

"I can manage, sir. If sleep is the concern, I can sleep in academic classes like other cadets. If academics are the concern, I can study during the evening study period. If punishments are the concern, I know that eventually the person punishing me will tire out, and it's just a matter of who gives up first, the person punishing me or me. And if my smile is the concern, I have never felt this happy in my life. Sir, DLTGH, today is the 39, and on the 40th day, I will be with my mother. I fear no man or senior. My smile is who I am," I said, wiping my face.

"That was a hell of a speech. You should have tried politics, but you are wrong about one thing. DLTGH, today is 40, not 39," he said, pointing out my mistake. I raised my right hand, pointed at his alarm clock, which read 0004H, and said,

"Sir, it has been four minutes since DLTGH 40 got over."

"Get up and get the hell out of my sight. Wake me up tomorrow at 0500H," he said.

I got up and ran towards my cabin. Finally, the dream of sleeping for more than four hours a day had become a reality.

In just a few short days, POP (Passing Out Parade) practices began. These practices marked the end of most of our events, including games and academics, and we were assigned to certain end-of-term activities. I was excited to be a part of the light and sound show, and I had practice twice a day. Life was comparatively easier now, and I couldn't wait to go home.

I remember that Saturday night, after the ante-room procedure, our SCC stood up and addressed us:

"Listen, you dimwits – DLTPO (Days left to Pass Out) today is 8, i.e. one week is left for us to pass out and you to go home. Let me tell you one thing, you all are the finest cunts I could have ever met. From today onwards, the fifth termers will run the squadron, and no sixth termer will touch you. It was a nice journey, and you all made it beautiful. I stand here on the part of all sixth termers, and I am proud that we had juniors like you. If we ever meet in the future - and we will meet - you are supposed to find me and take any treat from me. We depart today as seniors and juniors, but we shall meet next time as brothers. Respect the squadron. Keep your head high and do your best to make us proud. And remember, ONCE A BRAVE - ALWAYS A BRAVE."

With those words, all the sixth-termers got up, and we proceeded to the mess. One thing I particularly enjoyed about NDA was that all cadets had dinner together after the anteroom procedure. While dining that day, Sai said to me:

"Oyee.. Are you ready for tomorrow?"

"What's tomorrow?" I asked.

"Grudges Day - you idiot. The day I've been waiting for since the start of the term, tomorrow I'll have their asses," said Sai with a sly grin.

Grudges Day is a tradition in NDA where sixth-termers, after handing over their powers, can be punished by any junior in any way, and they have to oblige. It's a fun activity because, by this time, juniors have developed a unique love for their sixth-termers. I couldn't wait to see what Sai had planned for Grudges Day!

SUNDAY 1600H NEXT DAY

Squadron rumbled with a new announcement...

Pay Attention all Braves,

ALL SIXTHHH TERMERSSSS *SPRINT DOWN* TO... SALARIA LOBBYYYYY...

IMMEDIATELY IMMEDIATELY IMMEDIATELY

Hold up, my bad. The sprint down is only for our juniormost cadets, i.e. first to third termers. This announcement marks the start of GRUDGES DAY.

The sixth-termers were brimming with energy as they descended to the parade ground for their final punishment session in NDA. First to fourth termers wasted no time in dishing out all sorts of punishments like rolling, pushups, rope climbing, and more. To everyone's surprise, the sixth-termers tackled everything with a big smile.

It was then that I found myself standing face to face with my CSM, the Cadet Screwing Machine who had made our lives a living hell for the last 147 odd days.

"Start doing 1000 pushups, Bammel sir!" I said it to my CSM with utmost confidence.

"Brother, I never punished you this hard! Why are you seeking revenge?" replied Bammel sir, my CSM.

"It's karma, sir. What goes around comes around. Now, get to it!" I reiterated.

Bammel sir managed to do around 500 pushups when I finally told him to get up. I felt a pang of guilt watching him struggle. But to my surprise, he rose to his feet and said,

"Bhai, this is your last chance to take revenge. Don't waste it."

"Sir, I have no grudges against you," I said.

The torture continued for another hour before the sixth-termers finally got to dress up for the highly anticipated Squadron social.

An event called the "squadron social" was specially organized for the passing out course, where all officers and their significant others were invited. It was a night of endless dancing and merry-making, where cadets grooved to their hearts' content. As the clock struck midnight and everyone was sweating from dancing, the tired yet fulfilled cadets finally retreated to their cabins, ready for a well-deserved rest.

THE MELODY

Just as I was about to doze off, a loud kick on my cabin door jolted me awake. I turned around to find my overstudies standing there, their faces stern and unyielding. In unison, they barked at me, "Start rolling, you fucker!"

I was taken aback, wondering what I had done wrong in the last 24 hours. But without question, I started rolling, submitting myself to the brutal punishment that awaited me. For the next two hours, I was subjected to every kind of torment and agony I had endured throughout the term. By the time it was over, I was half-dead and drained of all energy.

Then, to my surprise, my overstudies took out a melody from their pockets and handed it to me. As they helped me up, they flashed me a smile and said,

"Smile, fucker. From today onwards, we are your pals."

In NDA, giving a melody to a junior is more than just offering candy; it is a symbol of friendship and camaraderie. From that moment on, my overstudies pledged to neither punish me nor allow anyone else to do so.

Filled with gratitude, I spent the next few days engaged in various activities, leading up to the big day (DLTGH 0). As the sixth-termers returned to the squadron with their parents, they brought sweets for us juniors. I eagerly ran from cabin to cabin, gobbling up as many treats as I could.

Eventually, I found myself outside my SCC's cabin, where he was packing his bags. Looking back on the 154 days of the term, I felt a sense of nostalgia and appreciation for all that I had learned and experienced. My SCC noticed me and extended his hand, saying,

"Thank you for everything, brother."

I spent some time with his parents before returning to my cabin to pack my bags.

As I reflected on how I had grown to respect and even love the seniors I had once despised, I made my way back to the parade ground, where a drill ustaad awaited me.

IT WAS THE TIME TO BOARD THE **NDA SPECIAL**!

5

Nda Special - The Wagon Of Dreams

But as fate would have it, Drill Ustaad discovered that three cadets were missing and began searching for them on the train. Upon our return, the Drill Ustaad confronted us, demanding an explanation.

"I was in the bathroom, Ustaad," Sharma replied calmly. "We had gone to the bathroom."

"All three at the same time?" the Drill Ustaad shouted in disbelief.

"Cadet abhi ghar nahi paucha hai aap - jaldi jaldi pair chaalao. Ese chalta hai jese park mai aaya ho.. makra cadet"

(Cadet, you haven't reached your home yet! Don't walk; start running! Don't walk as if you are in a park! You indolent cadet") shouted Drill Ustaad

For a moment, I felt like I was finally free from the shackles of NDA, but the drill ustaad's warning brought me back to reality. I hurried outside to see that all the cadets had already lined up before the squadron commander, and I immediately joined my coursemates. The Squadron commander gave us his best wishes and handed over our leave certificates.

We were then directed to a military bus that would take us to Khadki railway station, where the NDA Special awaited us. For those unfamiliar with it, the NDA Special is a special train service exclusively for NDA cadets and staff. Operated by Indian Railways, it ferries cadets and staff from various parts of the country to Pune and back. The train runs weekly, and its schedule is adjusted to coincide with the NDA's academic calendar.

The train is equipped with all necessary facilities for the comfort and convenience of the cadets and staff, including air-conditioned coaches, sleeper berths, a pantry car for catering, and dedicated security personnel. In case of emergencies, the train also provides medical facilities.

For an NDA cadet, the NDA special is a dream wagon. It's the train we've been waiting for since the start of the term - 154 long days. And let me tell you, it's a work of art.

When the bus finally arrived at the railway station, I expected to see an olive green NDA Special train waiting for us. I picked up our luggage, thinking that the term was finally over. But to my surprise, we were made to fall in again at the station. After a headcount, the adjutant was given a report, and all cadets were assigned their seat numbers. Drill ustaads were also tasked with monitoring our activities. What a pain, I thought to myself.

Finally, the NDA Special Train chugged along the tracks, making its way through the scenic countryside of India. Inside, the train was filled with young cadets from the National Defence Academy, all dressed in their crisp uniforms and looking eager and excited for the journey ahead.

As the NDA Special train sped towards their homes, the cadets settled into their seats and began to chat and joke with each other, filled with excitement. Some were old friends, and coursemates from the same squadron, while others were meeting for the first time. Despite this, they all shared the same emotion - the joy of returning home.

As the train journeyed on, the cadets took the opportunity to catch up on sleep, which had been deprived of them for the last few months. Occasionally, a cadet would wake up in a panic, thinking he was late for PT, only to realize he was on leave. But they would soon settle back into their seats, content to eat, borrow phones, and share stories with their coursemates. Others would wake up to find they had already missed their stop.

As the journey continued, we occasionally looked out of the window to see people amazed by the beautiful train passing by. This filled us with pride as we were part of the most prestigious academy in the country. When we grew tired of the routine, one of our coursemates proposed a plan to approach girls outside the train and ask for their phone numbers. It was a bold and risky plan, but we decided to execute it anyway.

The plan was simple - get off at Mathura junction, have a cup of tea, approach girls, and ask for their phone numbers. However, getting off the NDA special was strictly prohibited for cadets. To execute the plan, we had to ensure that Drill Ustaad was nowhere near. After much discussion, we decided to go for it. Three of us got off to buy chips while Rishi acted as our sentry.

But as fate would have it, Drill Ustaad discovered that three cadets were missing and began searching for them on the train. Upon our return, the Drill Ustaad confronted us, demanding an explanation.

"I was in the bathroom, Ustaad," Sharma replied calmly. "We had gone to the bathroom."

"All three at the same time?" the Drill Ustaad shouted in disbelief.

"What, Saab? It's a Nature's call. It can come anytime to anyone. Please use some logic," Sharma replied confidently.

Amazingly, the Drill Ustaad accepted our excuse and left without further ado. Though we had failed to approach any girls, it felt like a significant accomplishment for all of us. We had completed a successful mission - OPERATION CHIPS!

When the NDA special train reached Delhi station, we bid our coursemates goodbye and left for our respective homes, filled with memories of our journey together.

2200H THAT NIGHT

I approached my home, I could feel my heart beating faster with every step. It had been a while since I had last seen my family and I wasn't sure how they would react to my new appearance. I had not informed them about the exact day of my arrival, so they were not expecting me.

As I knocked on the door, I could hear my mom's voice from inside,

"Who is knocking the door this late at night?" Her voice was filled with concern and curiosity.

My mom opened the door and didn't recognize me at first. I had lost about 25 kgs of weight and was as thin as a stick. It took her a moment to realize who I was, and then she broke down. She hugged me and kissed my hands while tears streamed down her face. My dad had also joined her by this time, and we all three stood there crying together.

I had finally crossed the first gate. I was home!

gate 2:
the mysteries

6

Cross Country – The Pandemonium

As all the cadets gathered in the Salaria lobby on the ground floor, our cross-country captain was already there, ready to lead us. We had some sprouts and then went to the parade ground for warm-up. My heart was beating like a drum, and for a moment, I couldn't hear anything the seniors were telling me. I was lost in a different world, but then Rishi patted my back and said,

"Don't worry, I won't leave you behind. After all, you are my favorite girl. Haha, let's go now."

The first term break is a crucial period for every cadet. It serves as a refreshing pause and mentally prepares the cadet for the rigors of the upcoming term. For many, it is also the first time they leave the academy on leave, and they take pride in sharing their experiences at the NDA with friends and family. I remember my first term break vividly, and how I regaled my school friends with tales of my exploits at the academy, including a fabricated story about driving a tank!

After a well-deserved break, it was time to pack my bags and head back to the NDA. Although leaving my parents was a painful experience, I felt a sense of excitement knowing that I would now have junior cadets to mentor as a second-term cadet. Upon reaching Delhi station, the NDA special was waiting to transport me back to the academy. With a heavy heart, I bid farewell to my parents and embarked on a new journey.

Upon arriving at the NDA, I was pleased to see the new batch of first-term cadets. Looking at their innocent faces reminded me of my own first days at the academy, but this time I was an old hand. I could take on all the punishments with ease and quickly fell back into the NDA routine.

As a second-term student, I realized that life at the academy was no longer the easy ride I experienced in my first term. Gone were the days of easier tests and fewer activities. On the second day of the term, we were thrust into a rigorous schedule that felt all too familiar, with drill practice and cross country added to the mix. I had returned to the academy hoping for a better life, but instead found myself struggling to keep up. My precious little free time was consumed by cross country, leaving me exhausted and depleted. And just when I thought I couldn't take it anymore, I was expected to participate in drill practice in a comical rig known as the Games Rig Drill Order (GRDO) with my fellow coursemates.

Cross country, as they say in the NDA, is more than just a race. It's a "state of mind" that pushes cadets to their physical and mental limits. Whether you're a good or bad runner, the only thing that matters is your willingness to improve and do good for your squadron. Cross-country is not just a competition but a symbol of pride and honor. For juniors, failing to reach the finish line within the allotted time results in punishment, while for seniors, being outrun by a junior is a matter of self-respect.

I've seen people go mad for this event, with even the most rational and practical of cadets turning spiritual and sweating it out on the cross-country route to improve their timings by mere 10 seconds! I've seen people muttering about the event in their dreams, so intense is the excitement and anticipation.

But let me be clear, I hated running. Every cross-country route was torture for me. However, I appreciated a few things about this event, like juniors being allowed to wear watches to keep track of their timings and the respect and privileges a cross-country medalist would receive in the academy. A medalist wouldn't be punished by any seniors in his squadron, and the Alpha and Echo squadron would treat him like a sixth-term cadet, offering him special treatment.

Despite the pain of daily practice, with double routes even on Sundays, we persisted for two months. I lost weight, felt lighter, and ran faster, but it still wasn't enough. After every practice, seniors would force us to drink jugs of water to stay hydrated and massage our legs to avoid cramps. But finally, the day we had been waiting for had arrived.

The sun was setting on a Saturday evening as we stumbled back to our cabins, exhausted from our final practice run. Our cross-country captain stood up, a look of fierce determination in his eyes.

"Tomorrow," he said, his voice ringing out across the corridor, "is the day we've been training for these last two months. At 0600H, we'll stand at the start line, and by 0800H, there will only be one winner and 17 defeated squadrons. There is no second or third place for me. Tomorrow, if you feel like you're going to die, then die after you finish the run, or don't bother coming back to the squadron. I want you to run as if it's your last run. I want you to run like a brave."

We all knew that tomorrow would be the ultimate test of our endurance and spirit. But with those words ringing in our ears, we were ready to give it our all.

As the night before the final cross-country run came to an end, it was a tough one for everyone. The anticipation was overwhelming, and I tried my best to sleep, but all I could think about was the upcoming challenge. My mind was racing with a million thoughts, and I eventually dozed off.

The next thing I knew, it was 0400H, and I woke up thinking that I was the first one up. To my surprise, most of the cadets were already ready and eager to get started. Our cross-country captain was already in his sports gear, urging everyone to hurry up.

I quickly went to the washroom, brushed my teeth, and got dressed. As I was tying my shoes, my hands were shaking with fear. I tied the laces with two additional knots, securing them tightly, making sure they wouldn't come loose while running. The only thought that was going through my mind was that I couldn't be the reason for the squadron's loss.

As all the cadets gathered in the Salaria lobby on the ground floor, our cross-country captain was already there, ready to lead us. We had some sprouts and then went to the parade ground for warmup. My heart was beating like a drum, and for a moment, I couldn't hear anything the seniors were telling me. I was lost in a different world, but then Rishi patted my back and said,

"Don't worry, I won't leave you behind. After all, you are my favourite girl. Haha, let's go now."

Those words brought tears to my eyes, and I felt grateful to have such supportive coursemates. We started marching towards the start point, and the air was filled with excitement. We sang songs, clapped, and our seniors joined us. For that moment, nobody was a junior or senior. We were all brothers who shared a common bond—the Bravo Squadron.

The air was thick with anticipation and excitement as the cadets of the Bravo Squadron gathered at the start point for the cross-country run. The sun had just begun to peek above the horizon, casting a warm glow over the start point. The sound of shuffling feet and heavy breathing echoed throughout the area as the cadets bounced up and down to warm up their muscles.

The energy was electric as the cadets pumped themselves up for the grueling run ahead. The cross-country captain was at the forefront, his eyes fixed on the horizon with a steely determination. He barked out orders to the cadets, urging them to stay focused and push through the pain.

As the clock struck 0600H, the cadets took their positions at the start line. The tension was palpable as they waited for the signal to begin.

The adrenaline rush was overwhelming as each cadet mentally prepared themselves for the arduous task ahead.

The cross-country captain raised his hand, and in that moment, all was silent. The cadets held their breath, their hearts pounding with excitement. Then, the commandant raised a flag, and everyone started counting.

10,9,8,7,6,5,4,3,2 ....

With a sudden burst of energy, the captain lowered his hand and shouted, "Go!".

And just like that, the cadets took off like a pack of wild animals, their feet pounding the ground in unison. The sound of cheering and encouragement from fellow cadets filled the air, fueling their determination and resolve.

For a moment, it was like time stood still as the cadets sprinted towards the bottleneck (a point on the cross-country route), their faces set in grim determination. The excitement was overwhelming as they ran faster and harder than ever before, pushing themselves beyond their limits.

This was the moment they had been waiting for—the ultimate test of their physical and mental endurance. And as they raced towards the finish line, with sweat pouring down their faces and their hearts beating like drums, they knew that they had given it their all.

As the cadets approached the finish line of the cross-country, the energy in the air was palpable. The sound of cheers and claps from the spectators echoed through the trees, adding to the adrenaline rush that was already coursing through the runners' veins.

As the finish line came into sight, the cadets pushed themselves to their limits, determined to cross the line in the best time possible. The sight of the red ribbon marking the end of the grueling run spurred them on, and they sprinted towards it with all their might.

As each cadet crossed the finish line, their squadron mates erupted in a cacophony of cheers, congratulating them on a job well done. The sense of camaraderie was overwhelming, and it was clear that the bonds between the cadets had grown stronger through their shared experience.

Sweat poured down their faces, and their chests heaved with exhaustion, but the sense of accomplishment was all that mattered. Gasping for air, they tallied up the scores, eagerly trying to predict the winner.

BUT WHO WON THE GLIDER?

The Glider trophy was the stuff of legends, and only the squadron that had pushed themselves beyond their limits could hope to claim it. The Squadron that was united from start to finish, where every cadet—from the greenest rookie to the most seasoned veteran—was equally motivated and committed. It belonged to those who dreamed of nothing but lifting that coveted trophy high above their heads. Even as their injuries begged for mercy and their knees screamed in pain, they refused to give up. Those who kept running kept pushing and refused to let their breaths get heavier. Only those, my friends, were worthy of hoisting the Glider trophy high and mighty.

HE DIDN'T GIVE UP

I want to share a story about a remarkable coursemate of mine who I grew to admire after our first cross country. Running 14 kilometers takes a lot of motivation and perseverance, and this coursemate of mine was a fantastic runner. He always ranked in the top five of his squadron. However, on the final day of the cross-country, something unexpected happened.

In the last 2 kilometers, he broke his ankle. When I passed him on the route, I was shocked to see him. For an instant, I thought I was running too fast. But then, I saw him crying, and I realized something was wrong. Bound by the feeling to give points to my Squadron, I kept running.

But, did he give up because of a broken ankle? Absolutely not! He refused to let the injury hold him back and pressed on with unyielding determination. Each step he took was a testament to his sheer willpower. With gritted teeth and a heart of steel, he ran through the pain, determined to reach the finish line no matter the cost.

As the pain increased and he couldn't even stand properly, he started rolling towards the finish line. His back was bleeding from rolling, but he kept inching towards the finish line. And in the end, he emerged triumphant, his spirit unbroken, and his heart full of pride.

For this runner, giving up was never an option. His perseverance serves as an inspiration to us all, and I have the utmost respect for him. So, hats off to you, brother! You are a true inspiration, and your never-say-die attitude will forever be etched in my memory.

7

Camp Greenhorn

"Don't be a pussy. Understood? "If you try crying in front of me, I'll throw you out of the window," Sati said, trying to snap me out of it.

I managed to control my tears and shouted back at Sati, "What the fuck do you know about failing? You're a fake hero who likes to stay in the limelight. I'm from a public school and haven't received any special training like you. You know nothing about pain and how weakness eats your soul inside out."

"Sir, this is too much! I've already done almost 100 chin-ups today," Ahmad groaned, wincing with pain.

"Do ten more and move on to the ropes. We'll do the ropes 20 times, and then you can rest for two minutes," our PT captain said patiently.

After the cross-country run, we were subjected to even more physical training, and while everyone else rested on Sundays, our camp in-charge took us on grueling 20-kilometer runs with battle loads. Day by day, I began to feel more and more miserable. To make matters worse, I hadn't passed my DST

(Drill Square Test) like many of my other coursemates. Rishi, on the other hand, had passed on his first try and was excused from the drill practice in the evening before PT. I envied him. When we got rogered(punished) by our drill ustaad on the parade ground, he used to use that time to wash his clothes. During every evening study period, I was caught sleeping, which only resulted in more punishment from my corridor corporal (a fourth-term appointment).

Because of the cross-country run, many cadets lost their upper body strength and were subjected to harsh PT routines to make up for it. Time passed, and I eventually passed my PT test, but I was still stuck on my swimming test. The second-term swimming test involved swimming 50 meters, but I sank like the Titanic after only 30. I received even more punishment for failing, and it was the worst time of my life.

The day I came back after failing my swimming test, I was punished for several hours. I had started to fear water. When I returned to my room after getting punished by my CSM, Sati was waiting for me.

"You're a useless piece of sh*t." No, I correct myself—you're even worse. Because even sh*t floats!" Sati shouted.

Sati was good at everything. He was an ideal cadet—one of the fastest runners, a stud at PT, and a good student. Somehow, I was quite the opposite. Punishments didn't matter anymore. It was a matter of self-respect for me not to pass my tests on the first try. Sati's words broke the dam of tears I had been holding back. I tried to control myself, but I was already crying.

"Don't be a pussy. Understood? "If you try crying in front of me, I'll throw you out of the window," Sati said, trying to snap me out of it.

I managed to control my tears and shouted at Sati, "What the fuck do you know about failing? You're a fake hero who likes to stay in the limelight. I'm from a public school, and I haven't received any special training like you. You know nothing about pain and how weakness eats your soul inside out."

"I was the weakest of my batch once at Sainik School Ghodaghal," Sati said with a sigh. "But when someone ridiculed me, I worked extra hard and slept less at night to become better than the person mocking me."

I realized instantly that Sati's intent was not to humiliate people. Before I could say anything, he said, "Show me how you breathe in water."

For a moment, I thought he was crazy. But I followed his instructions like a loyal pet and laid on the tea table, imagining I was in the water. I showed him how I swam.

"See, that's the problem," Sati exclaimed, analyzing my swimming technique. "Your breathing isn't bad, but your leg kick needs work. Try to open up your legs as much as possible when you kick. Repeat that movement 1,000 times daily until your next swimming test attempt." With this said Sati left my cabin.

2 WEEKS LATER

As I emerged from the water, victorious in passing my swimming test, I couldn't help but feel a sense of overwhelming pride. It was all thanks to Sati's unconventional but effective teaching method. Who knew that lying on a teapoy table and imagining myself in water would be the key to my success?

But more than that, I had learned a valuable lesson: there is truly no substitute for hard work. All those days of grueling PT, endless chin-ups, and painful rope climbs had paid off. And now, with my DST and swimming test behind me, I could finally focus on the upcoming Camp Greenhorn.

For those unfamiliar with it, the Greenhorn Camp is a major milestone in the life of a cadet at the National Defence Academy (NDA). This four-day camp, organized by the Joint Training Team (JTT), marks the first time a cadet experiences field conditions and fieldcraft. The focus is on developing map-reading skills, communication procedures and instilling discipline and routine.

But as they say at NDA, "It's not the event that's difficult; it's the practice of that event that's difficult." And the camp practice was indeed challenging. Our days were filled with endurance runs and tent-pitching drills, while our nights were spent on night navigation exercises. I couldn't wait for the camp to be over.

Finally, the day arrived when we had to prepare for the camp. We loaded our tents, digging tools, and other supplies onto our backs and stood before our camp in-charge, who had invested much time and energy in us. Instead of motivating us, he said something that touched our hearts.

"I have been observing this squadron for the last two years, and no one has performed well in the camps. But I know you are a better course. It's time to prove that," he said.

With that, we set off for the Bombay stadium. As is customary, the camp starts with cadets marching from the stadium to the campsite, covering a distance of 18 kilometers in semi-mountainous terrain. This march is often called the Approach March at NDA. Upon reaching the site, I was immediately daunted by the barren, rocky land with no shade and the scorching sun beating down on us. After enduring punishments from our officer instructors, we were told we would have a tent-pitching competition, with only ten cadets allowed to participate. The allotted time for this exercise was 30 minutes, but every squadron completed it in just 15 minutes. Points were awarded based on various factors, such as timing, hygiene, and the standard of snake trenches and rain drains. Then, we were instructed to hold defenses in the area, which meant digging trenches.

The soil was as hard as a diamond, and most of our digging tools broke within two hours. As darkness fell, everyone became sleepy, and the pace of digging slowed. This was when the true test of camaraderie and loyalty to the squadron came into play. Everyone was frustrated, and no one wanted to work.

As exhaustion began to set in, Nikhil's brilliant plan offered a glimmer of hope.

"Let's work in shifts," he proposed. "Half of us can sleep while the others work, and the cycle can continue."

For a moment, I was hopeful for a good night's rest. But our dreams were quickly shattered by the bellowing voice of Harry.

"No fucker will sleep tonight!" he shouted. "What's the point of practicing so hard if we sleep tonight? Your asses can't even keep up for four days. Remember the promises you made to your seniors. Have some shame!"

At first, Harry's words stung. But then, a wave of electricity seemed to pass through my body, and I wasn't tired anymore. Without hesitation, I grabbed a shovel, my body moving automatically. I could sense that everyone else felt the same way. At that moment, a leader was born out of us.

> "Leaders aren't born. They are made. And they are made just like anything else, through hard work. And that's the price we'll have to pay to achieve that goal or any goal." — *Vince Lombardi.*

The sun was already up, but we were still digging, our hands and backs sore from the previous day's exertions. It was then that we received word that the Excercise Disha Gyan, or mini-josh, was fast approaching. The map readers among us started brushing up on their skills, preparing themselves to outdo one another in the upcoming test.

The mini-josh was a test of navigation skills, with all squadrons split into two groups and tasked with navigating different routes. The competition was fierce, with each checkpoint manned by Basic DS and every cadet given only a map and compass to find their way through the challenging course. Despite some getting lost due to poor navigation skills, everyone gave it their all and emerged exhausted yet triumphant.

The next day was packed with activities: MR tests, camp games, and plenty of ragda (punishment). But it was day four that truly put us to the test—the day of the Josh run.

The Josh Run was a grueling 20-kilometer race against time, with seven checkpoints to cross and our squadrons competing fiercely against one another. It was a true test of our physical and mental stamina, and we put our hearts and souls into every step. In the end, we came in second - a close call, but a victory nonetheless.

But the camp wasn't all about tough tests and competition. It was marked by a campfire, where we laughed and shared stories late into the night. And when we returned to our squadron, we were given a long mid-term mood—30 days of being treated like kings!

Looking back, it was undoubtedly one of the most challenging and rewarding experiences of our lives. And while the tests and trials of the academy were tough, they were nothing compared to the bonds we formed with our fellow cadets—bonds that would last a lifetime.

AUTHOR'S MESSAGE

"Greenhorn is not for the faint of heart. From day one, you'll be pushed to your limits—physically, mentally, and emotionally. You'll experience sleepless nights, grueling physical training, and mental challenges that will test your willpower. But it's all part of the process of becoming a strong and capable military cadet.

As you progress through the camp, you'll find that your camaraderie with your fellow cadets grows stronger each day. You'll work together to overcome obstacles and achieve your goals, forging deep bonds that will last a lifetime. The friendships you make at Greenhorn will be among the most meaningful and enduring of your life.

But the benefits of Greenhorn extend far beyond the friendships you'll make. This is where you'll learn to push yourself further than you ever thought possible, to embrace discipline and focus in a way that will benefit you throughout your military career. You'll emerge from Greenhorn stronger, more resilient, and better prepared for whatever challenges come your way.

So, embrace the toughness of Greenhorn, and use it to your advantage. This is your opportunity to become the best version of yourself, to rise to the challenges that lie ahead, and to make lifelong friends and memories along the way. It's not easy, but the rewards are worth it. **Are you ready to take on the challenge?"**

8

Liberty And Hockey!!

"What are you thinking?" he asked.

"Nothing. I have heard that the Hunters are very deadly and have injured many players in their previous teams," I said, my voice trembling with fear.

"What's there to worry about? If they hit you on your ankle, hit them in their face! It's that simple," said Panwar, his voice filled with confidence.

After the grueling Greenhorn, all that remained for us were the hockey and drill competitions. But we had earned the respect of our seniors, and our course was hailed as the best. It was the high point of our time at the academy, a period when we were free to indulge in some well-earned liberty and make new friends. I'll never forget my first taste of freedom.

Stepping outside the NDA, the air felt fresher, the absence of drill instructors and seniors more liberating, and most importantly, there were girls! For months, I'd grown bored of staring at the same male faces, and I couldn't wait to see what the opposite sex had to offer. On Sundays, we'd head to Gole Market, with barely any money to our names, and ogle at the girlfriends of other cadets and seniors, dreaming of a similar life.

Then the day came when I finally got to experience my first taste of liberty with my closest buddies. We waited at the Kondhwa bus stand, hoping for a ride into the city. Back then, there were no bus tickets to punch, and we barely had enough money to pay for our fare. So, we put our heads together and came up with a plan. Two of us would buy tickets, and then we'd pass them down the line, creating a cycle. By the time the conductor realized what we were up to, we'd be off the bus, laughing at our own cleverness.

Our plan worked for weeks until the conductor caught on to us. We managed to scrape together enough money to pay for the tickets that day, but the memory of our little chatki(smart act) still brings a smile to my face whenever I sit with my coursemates.

As the days passed, our preparations for the upcoming hockey and drill competition grew more intense. The atmosphere was electric, as every squadron in the academy was putting in their best efforts to come out on top. But for our squadron, it was more than just a competition. It was a chance to prove our mettle and to show everyone what we were truly capable of.

Playing games was always a fun activity for us, but this time it was different. We were driven by a fierce sense of determination to emerge victorious. And it was not just about winning; it was about pushing ourselves beyond our limits and discovering the strength that lay within us.

I had seen cadets who had never played a game before becoming masters of it through sheer grit and hard work. In the academy, every squadron had to make five teams, known as strings in the NDA. These strings were categorized as strings 1, 2, 3, 4, and 5, with the numbers denoting descending order of proficiency, with string 1 being the best and string 5 being those who didn't even know that a game of hockey involves a ball and a hockey stick.

I was a part of the second string, and our squadron was doing great in the competition. We had won all our matches except for one against the feared Hunter squadron, who played rough and aggressively. But we were not afraid. We were determined to give it our all, to put up a good fight, and to come out on top.

The day before the match was a Sunday and our team was given complete rest. I was washing my games rig in the washroom when my coursemate Panwar approached me.

"What are you thinking?" he asked.

"Nothing. I have heard that the Hunters are very deadly and have injured many players on their previous teams," I said, my voice trembling with fear.

"What's there to worry about? If they hit you on your ankle, hit them in the face! It's that simple," said Panwar, his voice filled with confidence.

Panwar was a tall and smart coursemate of mine from Meerut. He was a sportsman par excellence and had learned most of the sports at the academy itself. He was six feet tall, heavily built, and our main defender. No team had been able to get past him. He was our main line of defense—the wall, the one-man army.

His words brought some confidence to me, and I was ready to face the Hunters. It was a do-or-die situation for us, and we were determined to emerge victorious. The match would decide the winner, and we were ready for it.

MONDAY 1400H

As I wrapped up my academic classes for the day, I made a conscious decision to skip lunch. I had something much more important on my agenda - an evening game with my squadron team. Rushing back to the squadron, I was surprised to find my team captain already seated at the central stairs, all geared up and ready to go. I often wondered how he managed to beat me there every time.

Without wasting any time, my captain beckoned me over, "Hurry up, we have a big game to play."

I picked up the pace and headed straight to my cabin to change into my sports gear. Soon after, an announcement was made for the second-string team, and we all gathered on the ground floor.

Our captain stood up and addressed us, saying,

"I'm not the best at motivating people, but I can tell you this: This match will decide which squadron will lift the trophy. We both have equal points, so it's up to us whether we want to lift that trophy or not. Are you ready to hunt the hunters?"

In unison, we shouted back, "Yes, sir!"

Filled with adrenaline, we made our way to the playground, where the match was scheduled to begin at 1600H. As we arrived, we could see that the Hunters were already there, warming up. When I looked at their players, they all looked like they were ready to kill, their eyes bloodshot and their faces contorted in a menacing expression. It was clear that we were in for a tough game.

"Sir, these chickens are playing against us," Panwar quipped, laughing.

"Yes, Panwar. Let's show them what we've got," our captain replied confidently.

Watching Panwar in action was always an inspiration for me. He was fearless, a natural-born leader, and someone who always volunteered for everything. He started out as a rookie, but with his unwavering determination and confidence, he quickly rose to the ranks of a pro. Just being around him on the field was enough to boost my own motivation.

As we prepared to take on the Hunters, I couldn't help but feel a rush of excitement and anticipation. This was no ordinary game; it was a battle that would determine the fate of our squadron. But with our captain leading the way and Panwar by our side, I knew that we had what it took to emerge victorious.

> *I learned that courage was not the absence of fear but the triumph over it. The brave man is not he who does not feel afraid, but he who conquers that fear."* - Nelson Mandela.

In just a matter of minutes, the players were called to line up on the field. Standing alongside my captain and Panwar, I felt an overwhelming sense of camaraderie and determination. We were a team, united in our quest for victory, and we were willing to do whatever it took to achieve it.

As the referee blew the whistle, I could feel my heart rate quickening. This was it—the moment we had been waiting for. With every fiber of my being, I focused on the task at hand, blocking out all distractions and honing in on the game.

The sound of feet pounding against the grass filled the air as we charged forward, each of us fully committed to our respective roles on the field. It was a symphony of movement, with the ball passing between us like a well-choreographed dance.

As the game progressed, the tension mounted. The Hunters were proving to be formidable opponents, pushing us to our limits with their speed and agility. But we refused to give up, fighting tooth and nail for every inch of ground.

In the midst of it all, my captain and Panwar stood out as beacons of strength and leadership. Their unwavering confidence and strategic thinking kept us moving forward, even in the face of adversity.

As the game got underway, it was clear that both teams were evenly matched. The Hunters were relentless in their attacks, and we had to be at our best to keep up. But then, out of nowhere, my captain scored the first goal of the game, sending the entire squadron into a frenzy.

The momentum had shifted in our favor, and we were determined to hold on to the lead. But then disaster struck,

Panwar, one of our best players, was injured by an opponent's tackle. My blood boiled as I watched him writhe in pain on the ground.

But true to his character, Panwar refused to stay down. Despite his injury, he got back up and continued to fight, defending our goal with everything he had. It was an inspiring sight and only fueled our determination to win.

As the game entered its final stages, tensions were running high. The Hunters were pulling out all the stops, and we had to stay alert to defend our lead. But then, in a moment of frustration, I pushed a fifth termer who had been getting on our nerves. The referee wasted no time in showing me a yellow card, and I knew that I had let my emotions get the better of me.

But even that setback couldn't dampen our spirits. With Panwar back on the field, we fought with all our might, pushing ourselves to the limit. And when the final whistle blew, we knew that we had done it—we had emerged victorious, champions of the tournament.

As we celebrated our hard-fought victory, I couldn't help but feel a sense of pride in my team. We had faced adversity and come out on top—stronger and more united than ever before. And as we looked to the future, I knew that there would be many more battles to come, but I was ready, and I was honored to stand alongside my fellow soldiers, ready to do whatever it took to protect our country and defend our squadron.

9

Novices Boxing & The Academics Torch

"Suddenly, I felt something warm and wet running down my face. Blood was gushing out of my nose, and I could feel it trickling down my lips. I could hardly see my opponent, but I knew I had to keep fighting. I heard my seconds shouting at me to keep my guard up, but their voices seemed to be coming from a distance."

As the end of the term drew near, the anticipation in the air was electrifying. The academy was buzzing with energy as cadets prepared for the final activities, one of which was the novices' boxing competition. I had always been fascinated by boxing, but I had never actually set foot in a ring. The mere thought of it made my heart race with anxiety, but I was determined to leave my mark. I knew that the competition would be tough and that I would be fighting against some of the most skilled cadets in the academy, but I was determined to give it my all and show what I was capable of.

After being weighed, I was placed in the lightweight category, which meant I was to fight opponents weighing between 58-60 kilograms. We weren't given much time to practice; all we received were basic instructions on defense and attack. However, the stories our seniors told us about broken noses and teeth haunted me.

Every day, five cadets were nominated as seconds to help the fighter or carry them to the military hospital in case of injuries. Those who won bouts were complimented, while those who lost were usually punished. The opponent for each bout was decided by a random order that came in the afternoon order book.

The day of my bout arrived, and my seconds were Sharma and Tripathi. Instead of motivating me, they instilled fear in me by threatening punishment if I didn't win. Tripathi even gave me a can of Red Bull and joked that it would give me wings.

My opponent was a cadet from Kyrgyzstan, half my size but quicker and more agile. As the bell rang, I was ready to give it my all. My opponent was quick, but I didn't let that intimidate me. I was determined to show my seniors what I was made of.

The first round was tough. My opponent landed a few punches on me, but I managed to dodge most of them. However, in a moment of carelessness, he landed a hard blow to my ribs. I felt the pain shoot through my body, but I refused to let it slow me down. I gritted my teeth and kept on fighting.

The second round was even harder. My opponent had clearly studied my moves and was prepared to counter them. I could see the disappointment on the faces of my seniors as I struggled to keep up. I knew I had to do something to turn things around.

As we entered the final round, I took a deep breath and tried to focus. My opponent came at me with a flurry of punches, but I managed to dodge most of them. I landed a few punches of my own, but they didn't seem to have much effect. It was clear that I was going to lose the fight.

Suddenly, I felt something warm and wet running down my face. Blood was gushing out of my nose, and I could feel it trickling down my lips. I could hardly see my opponent, but I knew I had to keep fighting. I heard my seconds shouting at me to keep my guard up, but their voices seemed to be coming from a distance.

As the final bell rang, I collapsed on the floor. I was conscious, but barely. I could hear the sounds of my seniors rushing towards me, their voices full of concern. I tried to get up, but I was too weak. The next thing I knew, I was waking up in the military hospital.

I could feel the throbbing pain in my head, and I could barely open my eyes. My seniors were standing by my bedside, and they looked relieved to see me awake. They told me that I had put up a good fight against the national boxing champ of Kyrgyzstan, and commended me for my bravery. They praised my determination and resilience, and told me that I had made them proud.

Looking back on that day, I realized that it wasn't about winning or losing. It was about pushing yourself to the limit and showing what you were capable of. And in that moment, I knew that I had done just that.

As I made my way towards the exit of the hospital, I spotted Tripathi waiting for me, wearing his trademark grin. I couldn't help but wonder what he was up to.

"Hey man, how are you feeling?" he asked, still grinning.

"I'm feeling better, thanks for asking," I replied, still feeling a bit groggy from the medication.

"Good, good. Listen, about that Red Bull I gave you before the fight. You owe me a hundred bucks for wasting it," he said, his grin widening.

I rolled my eyes and chuckled, despite the pain that still lingered in my body. Tripathi was always cracking jokes, and I knew he was trying to lighten the mood after what had been a tough day for me.

"Alright, alright. You win," I said, shaking my head in disbelief.

Stepping out of the hospital, the evening breeze greeted us with open arms. And even though my body was bruised and battered, my spirit was anything but broken. In that moment, I felt a wave of triumph wash over me—a feeling I'd never experienced before. It wasn't about winning or losing; it was about pushing myself beyond my limits and proving to myself that I was capable of achieving more than I'd ever imagined.

As I looked up at the sky, I couldn't help but feel a sense of happiness wash over me. Another day had passed, and I had emerged victorious! The exhilaration of knowing that I had given it my all was overwhelming. It was a moment I would cherish forever—a moment of pure, unadulterated joy.

THE ACADEMICS TORCH

After the exhilaration of Novices Boxing died down, the real challenge began. Our semester exams loomed ahead, casting a shadow of dread over the academy. As a junior cadet, I quickly learned that everything at NDA was a disguised punishment. Even the month leading up to the end of term, which should have been a time of respite from drill competitions and POP practices, was filled with unrelenting academic pressure.

To make matters worse, the study periods were organized in the anteroom, where senior cadets kept a watchful eye to ensure that the junior cadets didn't fall asleep. It was a common sight to see cadets dozing off, and the punishment for such an offence was brutal. I remember one instance where a cadet had fallen asleep and kept rolling for hours before he finally woke up to study seriously.

On one such day, I found myself nodding off in the anteroom when I was rudely awakened by CSM Mehrotra's booming voice.

"Wake up, you fucker!" he barked. "While your seniors are sweating it out for the drill competition, you cunt want to sleep here?"

Before I could utter a word, he ordered me to "go get wet." I knew what this meant; it was a punishment that I dreaded. To get wet under a shower with clothes on and then continue the daily activities in wet clothes would result in rashes over the entire body.

As I was not allowed to enter the anteroom drenched wet, I was told to study outside. I made up my mind to control my sleep and study seriously this time. But my resolve was tested yet again when CSM Mehrotra caught me nodding off again.

"Fucker, you want to sleep again! How pathetic can you get? Go and study under the shower now!" he shouted.

I was studying under a shower, with water pouring over my head and my books getting wet! This continued for days until the exams were over, and finally, the end-of-term activities started.

After the exams were over, we were all assembled, and our CGPA, commonly known as a pointer, was declared. My heart was pounding as CSM Mehrotra began to call out the names of those who had failed in some subjects or who had scored a point less than 4. All of these cadets were punished for achieving this dubious feat.

Then came the moment of truth. The CSM announced the names of those who had achieved a pointer of 7.5 or higher, the academically elite known as "torchies". To my amazement, my name was called along with Sati, Sharma, and Tripathi. I had earned the right to wear the coveted academics torch, a symbol of excellence in the academy.

I was elated, but my joy was tempered by the memory of the punishing regime I had endured. Still, I couldn't help but feel a sense of pride as CSM Mehrotra grudgingly acknowledged my achievement.

"Thank God. You aren't as worthless as I thought," he muttered.

The end-of-term activities and the POP of the sixth termers came and went, and I was finally packing my bags for the term break. Looking back, I realized that **I had crossed the second gate of hell** and emerged stronger for it. The challenges I had faced had tested me to my limits, but I had persevered and triumphed. As I left the academy, I felt a sense of gratitude for the lessons I had learned and a determination to face whatever lay ahead with the same courage and resilience.

gate 3:

the pillars

10

Being A Dad Isnt Easy!

He was drenched in sweat, and suddenly he cried out in frustration.

"I can't take this monkey business anymore! This isn't what I signed up for! You make me do PT all the time, you punish me for trivial things, and you don't even care if I get hurt or injured. You don't have any feelings. You're a monster!"

The new term started off with a bang as we received new badges on our collars and greater power and authority. It was exhilarating to have more responsibility, but as the saying goes, with great power comes great responsibility. And with my newfound role as an overstudy, I had a new problem to deal with.

On the day we were assigned our understudies, I couldn't help but feel a little apprehensive. As third termers, we were tasked with guiding and training the first termers. I remember scanning the crowd of new cadets, hoping to find someone who was already physically and mentally fit—someone who would make my job easier. But as fate would have it, my luck had run out. My understudy turned out to be a thin and timid boy named Dabral.

I could see the fear in his eyes as I approached him. He looked like a lost kitten in a new and unfamiliar world. I couldn't help but wonder how I would ever be able to train him. As a third-termer, I had always dreamed of having a RIMCOLIAN or GEORGIAN as my understudy—someone who was already trained and would pass all their tests without any extra effort. But that wasn't the case with Dabral. He was the exact opposite of what I had hoped for.

RAISING A REBELLIOUS SON

Training Dabral was like raising a rebellious son. At first, he revolted against everything I tried to teach him. It reminded me of my own first termer days, when I was equally stubborn and headstrong.

Dabral was always questioning my authority, pushing the boundaries, and testing my patience. He was constantly challenging me and questioning the rules and regulations of the academy. I knew I had my work cut out for me if I wanted to turn him into a disciplined soldier.

I started by teaching him the basics of academy life: the mess etiquette, the routines, and the protocols. I tried to instill in him a sense of discipline and order, but he resisted every step of the way. It was frustrating sometimes, but I was determined to make him the best first-termer.

I knew that part of the reason he was so rebellious was because he felt lost and confused. He was in a new and unfamiliar environment, and he didn't know how to navigate it. So I decided to take him under my wing and show him the ropes.

I spent hours with him every day, teaching him everything I knew about the academy. Slowly but surely, I started to see a change in him. He was becoming more disciplined, more focused, and more committed to his training.

But just when I thought he had finally turned a corner, he would revert back to his old ways. He would push back against my authority and resist my instructions. It was like taking one step forwards and two steps back.

As an overstudy responsible for training Dabral, I encountered situations where it was necessary to discipline him for his mistakes. Seeing him in pain and crying brought back memories of my own experiences as a first-termer. It was a mixture of pity and responsibility that drove me to make him a competent cadet, even if it meant being tough on him at times. One instance that stands out in my memory is when I was disciplining him at 0200H in the dead of night. He was drenched in sweat, and suddenly he cried out in frustration,

"I can't take this monkey business anymore! This isn't what I signed up for! You make me do PT all the time, you punish me for trivial things, and you don't even care if I get hurt or injured. You don't have any feelings. You're a monster!"

His words stung me, but I knew that I was doing my job correctly. I patiently observed him without saying a word. I could see he expected punishment, but instead, I turned my back on him and pretended to sleep. It was a tactic that I learned from my overstudy. It was a form of mental torment.

After two long hours, Dabral grew impatient and broke down in tears. Then I left him to prepare his cabin for tomorrow's cabin cupboard inspection!

CABIN CUPBOARD – SON VS FATHER

Cabin cupboard inspection at the National Defence Academy is a highly anticipated event that keeps every cadet on their toes. It's a meticulous process where every nook and cranny of a cadet's living space is inspected to ensure that it's in perfect order. From the neatly arranged clothes in the cupboard to the polished shoes under the bed, every detail is scrutinized. It's a test of discipline and attention to detail, and one that every cadet takes seriously.

It was the night before the cabin cupboard inspection at the National Defence Academy, and tensions were running high. Dabral, was particularly nervous, as this was his first time being inspected. I tried to calm him down and help him prepare, but he was so anxious that he could barely think straight.

Despite my efforts, the next day, Dabral's cupboard was a complete mess. His bedsheet, which was supposed to be pristine white, was covered in dirt and stains. I was so angry and disappointed, as I had tried my best to help him prepare. But instead of being grateful, he made a mess of everything.

As his overstudy, I was responsible for ensuring that the cabin was in order. But because of Dabral's negligence, I was punished for days, tarnishing my reputation. I felt humiliated and betrayed, and I knew that I had to teach Dabral a lesson.

I confronted him about the incident, and he initially denied any wrongdoing. But eventually, he confessed to intentionally spoiling his bedsheet as revenge for my strict training methods. He felt that I was too hard on him and that I didn't understand his struggles.

I was furious at his insolence and lack of respect, and I punished him severely. I made him run extra laps and do push-ups until he was exhausted. I wanted him to understand that there were consequences for his actions and that he couldn't just do whatever he wanted.

As I stood there, punishing Dabral for his mistake, a wave of regret washed over me. He was just a young cadet, trying to navigate the challenges of the academy. In many ways, I could empathize with his struggles. But as a senior cadet, I had a duty to enforce the strict rules and regulations of the academy, no matter how harsh they might seem. And so, I continued disciplining him, hoping he would learn from his mistakes and become a better cadet. The rivalry between us, akin to that of a father and son, had begun!

11

The Responsibility!

"I just can't seem to get it right," he said, his voice full of despair. "I'm not cut out for this."

I looked at him steadily, my gaze firm but kind.

"You are cut out for this," I told him. "You just need a little bit of guidance and support."

In the hallowed halls of the academy, the third termers hold a special place of honor. They are the pillars upon which the future of the squadron is built, responsible for shaping the raw clay of new cadets into the best officers they can be.

Their duty is no small task. The future of the squadron rests on their shoulders, and they take this responsibility with pride and determination. With each passing day, they pour their hearts and souls into the development of the new cadets, imparting upon them the wisdom and skills necessary to succeed in the rigors of the academy environment.

The third-termers are the ones who mold the future leaders of the squadron. They know that the cadets under their tutelage will one day be the ones who will run the squadron, taking it to new heights of success and glory. And so, we approach our task with love and care, nurturing each cadet like a parent would their child.

To be a third-termer is to be a beacon of hope, a guiding light for those who are just starting their journey at the academy. It's a role that is both challenging and rewarding, one that requires discipline, dedication, and a deep sense of responsibility.

And yet, despite the challenges, the third termers approach their duties with a sense of joy and enthusiasm. For them, there is no greater satisfaction than seeing their cadets succeed and knowing that they had a hand in shaping the future of the squadron.

When Dabral arrived at the academy as a new cadet, he was like a fledgling bird, unsure of his place in the world. But as his senior cadet and mentor, it was my responsibility to take him under my wing, and from that day forwards, he was on my charge.

I took this responsibility seriously, knowing that every mistake he made reflected not just on him but on me as well. When he struggled with his academics or fell ill, it was my duty to help him recover and get back on track. When his room was a mess or he struggled with discipline, I was there to guide him and set him on the right path.

But my responsibilities went beyond just his physical and academic well-being. It was my duty to shape him into the best cadet he could be, to teach him the values of discipline, courage, and honor. It was my job to instill in him the leadership qualities that would one day make him a great overstudy, and to help him develop the skills he would need to succeed in the academy and beyond.

Being responsible for Dabral was a weighty task, but it was also a labor of love. Watching him grow and develop under my guidance was one of the most rewarding experiences of my time at the academy. And though there were times when it was challenging, I wouldn't have traded the experience for anything in the world. Because being a mentor and guide to someone like Dabral was what being a cadet was all about.

As the days passed, Dabral struggled with some of the most basic requirements of the academy. His PT tests were poor, and he found himself struggling to keep up with his peers during swimming exercises. I watched as he grew increasingly frustrated and disheartened, knowing that it was my responsibility to help him overcome these challenges.

One day, after another poor PT session, I approached Dabral and asked him what was going on.

"I just can't seem to get it right," he said, his voice full of despair. "I'm not cut out for this."

I looked at him steadily, my gaze firm but kind.

"You are cut out for this," I told him. "You just need a little bit of guidance and support."

Together, we went over the PT exercises, and I showed Dabral how to do them correctly, encouraging him to focus on his form. We spent countless hours on the ground, practicing until Dabral's movements were fluid and precise.

And when it came to swimming, I knew that Dabral needed a different approach. "It's all about technique," I explained to him, as we stood by the edge of the pool.

"You don't have to be the strongest swimmer, but you need to be efficient."

For weeks, we worked together, with me guiding Dabral through the motions, correcting his form, and offering words of encouragement. Slowly but surely, his swimming improved, and he began to feel more confident in the water.

The day of his PT and swimming tests arrived, and I watched nervously as Dabral stepped onto the field and into the pool. But this time, he looked different - he looked confident, focused, and determined.

As he completed his PT exercises, I saw a marked improvement in his form and technique. He moved through the drills with ease, his breathing steady and controlled.

And when it came to swimming, I watched as Dabral glided through the water, his movements fluid and efficient. He swam faster than I had ever seen him swim before, and I knew that he had finally found his rhythm.

When it was all over, Dabral emerged from the pool, dripping with water and beaming with pride. I clapped him on the back, feeling a sense of satisfaction knowing that I had helped him achieve this success.

"Thank you," he said, his voice filled with gratitude. "I couldn't have done it without you."

"Come on, you think you can just smile and say thank you? What happened to your basics?" I barked, trying to maintain a stern demeanor.

I ordered him to do 28 creamrolls and a 100 pushups as punishment. To my surprise, he completed them all with determination and grit.

As he stood up, a wide grin stretched across his face.

"Thank you, I couldn't have done it without you," he said.

That's when it hit me—this wasn't the same Dabral I had known just a few months ago. He wasn't afraid of punishment anymore; he was ready for his moment to shine. Our old father-son rivalry was a thing of the past.

12

A Cadet's Curse – The Rejection!

"Go talk to her," Sharma urged me.

My heart was racing, and my palms were sweaty as I walked over to her.

"Hi, can I join you?" I asked, hoping she wouldn't think I was too forward.

She looked up from her book and smiled at me. "Sure," she said.

The third term at the NDA was coming to an end, and I couldn't wait to go home. Being away from family for months on end was starting to take a toll on me, and I longed for the comfort of my own home. However, something else was also starting to weigh heavily on my mind - my inability to approach girls on liberty.

Whenever we were allowed to leave the academy for a few hours, my eyes would roam over every girl I saw, admiring their beauty and grace. But when it came to actually approaching them, I would always chicken out at the last moment. I was too shy and afraid of rejection to take the plunge.

My coursemates noticed my reluctance and decided to give me a push.

"Come on, man, you're in the prime of your youth. You can't just let these opportunities pass you by," they would say.

I knew they were right, but I just couldn't seem to shake off my fear.

On every liberty, I would develop an attraction for a new girl. There was the girl at the coffee shop with the warm smile, the one at the bookstore with the twinkling eyes, and the one at the park with the infectious laugh. Each one seemed perfect in its own way, and I would fantasize about spending time with them.

One day, while on liberty, I spotted a girl sitting alone at a table outside a cafe. She was reading a book and sipping on a cup of coffee, and something about her caught my eye. I felt drawn to her, and my coursemates noticed my interest.

"Go talk to her," Sharma urged me.

My heart was racing, and my palms were sweaty as I walked over to her.

"Hi, can I join you?" I asked, hoping she wouldn't think I was too forward.

She looked up from her book and smiled at me. "Sure," she said.

We struck up a conversation, and I found myself laughing and enjoying her company. Her name was Rhea, and she was studying literature at a nearby college. We had a lot in common, and before I knew it, it was time to head back to the academy.

Over the next few weeks, Rhea and I became inseparable. We would meet up on every liberty, explore the town, and talk for hours on end. I had never felt so comfortable around anyone before, and I knew that I had found a true friend in her.

But just as I was starting to feel like everything was falling into place, a plot twist rocked my world. Rhea had a boyfriend, and she revealed that she was only interested in being friends.

At first, I was disappointed, but I knew that I had to respect her decision. I valued her friendship too much to risk losing it by trying to push for something more. We continued to hang out, and our friendship only grew stronger.

Reflecting on my journey, I realized that my fear of rejection had held me back for far too long. But if I hadn't confronted that fear, I would never have met Rhea, the girl who would become my closest friend and confidante.

As our final events came to a close, I wrapped up my duties as an overstudy and watched as Dabral received the coveted melody after a grueling four-hour ragda session. As I packed my bags for the NDA special train, I couldn't help but feel a sense of relief and anticipation. Half of my training at NDA was over, and I was finally heading home.

But as I looked ahead to the next term, I couldn't help but feel a twinge of worry. The upcoming term was notorious for being the most difficult one at NDA, and I knew that I would need to give it my all to succeed. Despite this, I refused to let my fears get the best of me. I was determined to approach the next term with hope and enthusiasm.

With a big smile on my face, I marched off towards the NDA special, ready to return to the academy as a fourth termer – the Joshbox of the academy.

gate 4:
the Joshbox!

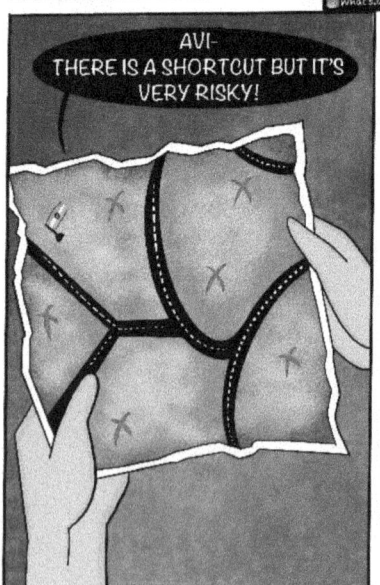

13

The Breaking Point

"What do they think we are? Prostitutes?" shouted Kumar. "They keep working us day and night and expect us to be perfect. This isn't a squadron; it's a brothel! I swear, one day, I'll kill that CSM bastard."

"Hey, Kumar, when you do it, make sure to give him two kicks on my side too," said Rishi with a laugh.

"Five nights of no sleep and a heavy load on our backs?" "Is this some military training or torture?" grumbled Rishi, struggling with his 25 kg load.

Panwar hissed back, "Keep quiet, or the CSM will make it five more nights for you."

I stood with the other fourth-termers, all of us weighed down by heavy loads on our backs. The corridor felt never-ending, and our bodies ached from the punishment we had endured for the past five days. Some of us tried to catch some sleep while standing, while others struggled to maintain balance under the weight of their loads. It was a grueling experience that we just wanted to be over with.

But the CSM wasn't done with us yet.

"You think you can talk back after just one week in the academy? Add two more bricks to your rucksacks!" he bellowed from his cabin.

We rushed outside, added the bricks, and returned to the same spot. Our ODT was just over an hour away, and we hoped that the punishment would end soon. But then the CSM came out and inspected our rucksacks.

Ahmad, thinking he could get away with not adding the bricks, was caught red-handed. The CSM was livid.

"You think you're too smart? You'll report to me for another five nights, and it's all thanks to your friend here," he said, pointing at Ahmad.

I wanted to lash out at Ahmad for making things worse, but Harry gave me a warning look. It was clear that this was just the beginning of hell, and we needed to learn to work together and endure whatever challenges came our way.

Over the next few nights, I tried every trick in the book to escape the pain and exhaustion of the punishing routine. However, the one thing that became my constant companion was the door to my CSM's cabin. I studied every detail of it—the brown paint that had lost its luster, the brass knob that had three screws, and the tiny drops of white paint that had accidentally splattered on it while painting the side walls.

I even noticed that one of the screws on the brass knob was black, and I couldn't help but wonder why. It was as if I had fallen in love with the door and the details of its design. But, of course, if only I could apply this level of attention to a girl, she would surely fall for me. For now, though, I had to settle for my love affair with the door!

The days were just as grueling. As fourth-termers, we were expected to run the squadron, ensuring that juniors were always in the right place, at the right time, and in the right rig. Any mistake made by a junior meant punishment for us. We were responsible for everything, and it felt like we had to do everything.

But amidst the grueling demands of the academy, there were a few small things that made the fourth term a little more bearable. We were no longer subjected to public humiliation or punished in front of everyone. Our punishment rigs had been upgraded, and we were given a level of respect in front of our juniors. These privileges may seem insignificant to most people, but to us, they were a beacon of hope and a glimmer of joy in an otherwise challenging experience.

After 18 months of rigors training, discipline, and hard work, we had finally earned the right to these privileges. We could finally latch our cabins at night, wear our socks in a certain way to show off our stripes, and even buy our own music system. I still remember going to the gole market to purchase my own music system and setting it up in my cabin with great pride, even though we hardly ever had time to use it. It was a dream come true and a symbol of our hard work and dedication.

I felt emotional on the day we were issued our white patrols, which would be the uniform we would wear on our passing out day. I would keep it carefully wrapped to keep it shining like white marble, as it was the most esteemed possession of my life. However, life was far from easy. We were in charge of everything, from cross-country practice to games, and we had to set an example for our juniors in every aspect of our lives.

We had to work extra hard to pass our physical and swimming tests on the first attempt, and lead the squadron in cross-country runs. The burden of responsibility was heavy, and it weighed heavily on us.

It was just another Saturday at NDA, and while the juniors were off watching a movie, we fourth termers were enduring yet another three-hour punishment. This was a routine occurrence for us, and we had come to expect it every weekend. The rare Saturdays when we were allowed to go to the movies meant that the fifth termers were getting punished. But for us, it wasn't the movie that we longed for. No, it was the chance to sleep uninterrupted for three blissful hours!

I remember one Saturday, about two months into the term, when we were called to report to a senior. As we gathered, our frustration with the constant punishments boiled over into angry words.

"What do they think we are? Prostitutes?" shouted Kumar. "They keep working us day and night and expect us to be perfect. This isn't a squadron; it's a brothel! I swear, one day, I'll kill that CSM bastard."

"Hey, Kumar, when you do it, make sure to give him two kicks on my side too," said Rishi with a laugh.

"Make that two for me as well," chimed in the rest of us.

Even though we were all exhausted and pushed to our limits, we found humor in the situation. Punishments had become a bonding experience, something that brought us closer together. We were willing to fight and even die for each other.

After each punishment session, my coursemates would come to my cabin. I always kept a good stock of supplies, so we would cook Maggi noodles on an iron and eat it with our hands, spreading the hot noodles onto newspapers. It was a simple meal, but it brought us comfort and camaraderie.

As challenging as those initial days at NDA were, they ultimately brought us together and made us stronger. We were constantly kept on our toes, between enduring punishments and frantically running around the squadron. Time seemed to pass by at a snail's pace.

I can still recall a defining moment when we stood outside Raj's cabin, a sixth-termer who had made our lives a living hell. It was 0200H, and we were weighed down with our usual loads, chatting amongst ourselves without a hint of fear. We had already experienced the worst of what NDA had to offer and were curious to know what else could be thrown our way.

Suddenly, Raj emerged from his cabin and uttered the words:

"I think you assholes are now ready for your ROVERS!"

14

Rovers

Avi studied the map, scratching his head and turning it around to find a solution. "We only have 12 kilometers to go, and we've lost 2 hours. But if we take this re-entrant," he pointed to the map, "we can cut one hour off our time. It's risky, though."

"How risky? "Are we going to die if we take that route?" asked Harry.

The challenge of Camp Rover is one of the most demanding and prestigious tests for every NDA cadet. For five grueling days, the cadets of the fourth term are put to the ultimate test of endurance, grit, and determination. The emphasis is on night exercises, which involve long marches through treacherous terrain and taking shelter in bivouacs during the day. Sleepless nights are followed by lectures and demonstrations on camp-related aspects, briefing and debriefing of exercises, and intense preparation for the next round of night exercises.

But Camp Rover is more than just a test of physical endurance. It is a test of character, leadership, and initiative.

The cadets are forced to push beyond their limits, both mentally and physically, and rely on their training and each other to survive. The bonds of camaraderie are strengthened, and the spark of initiative is ignited in each cadet.

Approach March was our first test of Camp Rover. It was a 18-kilometre night march from NDA to the campsite over hilly terrain full of thick vegetation. Squadrons were left as one entity at an interval of 10 minutes each, and the march took almost 8-9 hours to complete. Before the camp even started, we were pushed to our limits, with endurance runs of 20-40 km every Sunday, followed by night navigation exercises under the watchful eye of our camp in-charge Raj.

For a teenager, Camp Rover is a test of faith and confidence in themselves and their capabilities. It's an initiation rite of passage from boys to men, and every cadet who completes it can be proud of their achievement.

"How much longer do we have to endure this?" Kumar groaned in pain after walking for four hours.

"Only about one-third of the way there," the Ustaad replied, trying to break us mentally.

Kumar's sarcastic response only added fuel to the fire.

"Wow, that's great news, Ustaad! Harry just told me we have another 40 kilometers to go. Such a relief!"

Despite the weight of our battle load, it felt like a schoolbag compared to the last two months of Ragda. The long nights of punishment had paid off, strengthening us both physically and mentally.

Upon arrival at the campsite, the exercise bivouac pitching began, and we got to work with full zest. We pitched our bivouacs, dug snake trenches, and established fire points and armory, all according to the camp procedures.

Then we were put into exercise Pareeksha, and I knew we were in for a challenging experience. This grueling test was aimed at assessing our map reading skills, both written and practical, with grades reflected in a portion of our academic studies. But that was just the beginning.

Next up was a survival lecture. I'll never forget the rush of excitement as we were given a first-hand experience in these survival techniques, even going so far as to drink snake's blood and sample delicacies like frogs and lizards.

Of course, it wasn't all fun and games. In between these activities, ragda was like a default, leaving us rolling bareback for hours on end and depriving us of sleep. But honestly, we had seen worse, and all of these challenges seemed like a piece of cake.

Finally, after the campfire on the last night of camp, we were granted a brief respite of 2-3 hours of rest. It was like a dream come true, but little did we know that this rest was given to prepare us for the final test: the Josh run.

HOWS THE JOSH? - NOT SO HIGH SIR!

The Josh Run was the ultimate test of navigation and endurance— a 40 kilometer march across rugged, hilly terrain. The event started in the evening, far from the campsite. We were pumped up and determined to outdo our previous performances.

We were leading the pack as we sprinted through the pitch-black night, navigating from one checkpoint to the next. But at our fifth checkpoint, our map reader, Avi, made a grave error. Instead of following the map, he took a shortcut based on his intuition, which cost us a 2-hour penalty and an additional 20 kilometers. We were devastated, and Avi broke down in tears, taking full responsibility for our setback.

But Harry, our spirited coursemate, stepped up to motivate us.

"What's the use of crying over spilt milk, Avi? You guided us accurately through the previous four checkpoints. We're proud of you. Now, pick up that map, and let's find a shortcut. We can still do this!"

Harry's words reignited our determination. Avi studied the map, scratching his head and turning it around to find a solution.

"We only have 12 kilometers to go, and we've lost 2 hours. But if we take this re-entrant," he pointed to the map, "we can cut one hour off our time. It's risky, though."

"How risky? "Are we going to die if we take that route?" asked Harry.

"No, but..." Avi hesitated.

"Then it's done." "We're going through this motherfucking re-entrant," Harry declared with determination.

We entered the re-entrant, determined to succeed. We ran with reckless abandon, slipping and falling as we made our way down the hill. But we refused to give up. We had found a new hope, a renewed sense of purpose that kept us pushing forward.

THE CALAMITY

While we were running like wild horses, I suddenly heard a clicking noise. The next thing I knew, I was lying on the ground, my knee twisting in the opposite direction. A sharp pain ran down my spine, and tears started rolling down my face. I tried to get up, but I fell again. Harry came over to help, taking out his jackknife and tearing my trousers. My knee was swollen like a balloon, and every movement was excruciatingly painful.

Just when I thought I couldn't go on, Sharma spoke up.

"Don't give me the excuse of a broken knee," he shouted. "Get up and run these last few miles. If you can't lift the load, I'll carry it for you. If you can't run, tell me, and I'll lift you on my shoulders. But don't give up now!"

With Sharma's words ringing in my ears, I found a renewed sense of strength. He wrapped my knee tightly with a crepe bandage, and Rishi gave me some painkillers. I took three pills and soon felt a wave of relief wash over me.

With Harry and Sharma holding my arms and Rishi pushing me from the back, we started running faster than before. We were determined to finish what we had started, no matter what.

By the time I came back to my senses, the Josh Run, Firing, and Obstacle Course were over, and we had emerged as the overall runners-up in ROVERS.

COURSEMATES WILL DIE FOR YOU!

Coursemates by your side,

Through thick and thin they'll abide,

Training hard, with sweat and tears,

Growing stronger through the years.

In the academy you'll find,

Friends who'll have your back in mind,

Coursemates who will die for you,

Loyal, brave and ever true.

In the heat of battle's fight,

Coursemates stand with all their might,

Brothers and sisters in arms,

Protecting you from all harms.

So cherish every moment spent,

With those who'll be there 'til the end,

Coursemates who will die for you,

Forever faithful, strong, and true.

15

Drill Competition

After four weeks of bed rest, I was finally able to walk without any support, but the only way to fully heal was through knee surgery and six months of complete rest. However, this also meant that I would be relegated, and I couldn't afford to lose a term. I was torn between enduring the pain and continuing the term or getting the surgery and risking relegation.

After returning from our grueling Rovers camp, we were met with a warm embrace from Raj, who congratulated us on our achievement. Despite our tattered clothes and exhausted state, Raj ordered a feast from the gole market to replenish our energy. We indulged in the delicious food and then rested, grateful for the respite.

As for me, Raj carried me on his back to my cabin, where Dabral, my understudy, who had completed Camp Greenhorn, awaited my arrival. Dabral helped me change, took me to the shower, and made my bed, ensuring that I was comfortable. He then brought snacks from the market and kept them within reach. I slept for a whopping 36 hours, with Dabral waking me periodically to feed and check on me.

However, when I finally awoke, I was struck with a sharp pain in my knee, and I struggled to walk. The fear of permanent injury and the possibility of never running at full speed or doing jumps again hit me hard, and I broke down in tears. Two hours later, my coursemates carried me to the Military Hospital, where the diagnosis was a complete ACL and PCL tear in my knee, requiring immediate hospitalization.

DILLEMA?

The notion of being admitted to the hospital was frowned upon among cadets, as it was seen as a sign of giving up and seeking refuge in a place of safety. But for me, staying at the Military Hospital was a welcome respite from the grueling physical training and classes. I had good breakfasts and slept soundly, but with each passing day, I lost my physical fitness and respect among my squadron.

After four weeks of bed rest, I was finally able to walk without any support, but the only way to fully heal was through knee surgery and six months of complete rest. However, this also meant that I would be relegated, and I couldn't afford to lose a term. I was torn between enduring the pain and continuing the term or getting the surgery and risking relegation.

One day, while doing pushups in the hospital, I was startled by a loud voice. It was my squadron commander, standing in uniform, looking at me with a quizzical expression.

"So, you're having quite a fun time here," he remarked, but his tone was not condescending.

"F-fine, sir," I stuttered, struggling to hold back tears.

"Show me how you walk," he ordered.

I tried to walk, pushing through the pain, but I fell after a few steps. He observed me for a moment and then spoke firmly, "You need to strengthen your quads! Start doing quad sets and heel slides. It might hurt in the beginning, but I'll help you. Now pack everything and come with me to the squadron. I've already spoken to the doctor. If you stay here, you'll miss your semester exams and be relegated, and I can't let that happen."

On that day, I realized that my squadron commander wasn't the monster I thought he was. Though he used to punish us often, it became clear to me that there was a reason behind his actions. Deep down, he cared for us like his own children.

Filled with this newfound understanding, I packed my bag and marched off to the squadron where my coursemates were sweating it out for the drill competition. As they saw me, they came running towards me with their drill shoes, making all kinds of weird noises. But, the real problem was the CSM waiting for me. Upon seeing his face, I knew I was going to do all sorts of punishments, and with my broken knee, I wondered how I'd endure them. But, to my surprise, he said,

"Go change and make sure the juniors are studying properly for the exams. You will not be participating in the drill competition or any activity that might aggravate your injury. And don't think I like you or something. You are still useless to me. Now get going, and let me practice."

I was shocked at his kindness. Was I dreaming? But, I soon realized that the squadron spirit tied all cadets together. A senior might punish you and make your life a living hell, but they wouldn't let anyone touch you outside the squadron.

Over the next few days, I engaged in all sorts of minor tasks, from applying Brasso to buttons to stitching white patrols to making juniors sit for study periods. Meanwhile, my coursemates practiced drills for 4-6 hours every day, and the practice was intense. I watched as my seniors and coursemates lost weight every day, practicing in the afternoon and at night, trying to synchronize every movement. The sight filled me with a sense of pride. The CSM shouted at the top of his lungs to perfect his commands, and the contingent marched like a dolphin swimming in water. The rhythm set by my seniors and coursemates looked like a perfect song.

Finally, the day arrived for the drill competition. Like all the other squadrons, we did our best, but Charlie Squadron emerged as the winner, maintaining their tradition of winning the competition again!

The next few days were full of POP practices, and finally, it was the day everyone packed their bags to go home.

FAREWELL TO A FRIEND: WHEN THE NEST EMPTIES AND THE BIRD FLIES AWAY"

As the fourth term came to an end, I found myself sitting in my evil overstudy's cabin, feeling a mix of emotions. He had been the same jerk who had made my initial days at the academy miserable, but now seeing him leave was bittersweet. I struggled to find the right words to express myself, but before I could, he spoke up.

"So, you're a fifth-termer now. I can't believe a piece of sh*t like you made it this far," he said with a sly grin.

"Even I can't believe an asshole like you made it to the end and is passing out today," I retorted, fighting back tears.

We both laughed and then he said something unexpected.

"I'll miss you, bro," he said, holding out his hand for a shake.

I was taken aback for a moment, but then I firmly gripped his hand.

"I'll miss you too, sir," I said, surprised at the warmth in my own voice.

Leaving my overstudy's cabin, I felt a wave of emotions wash over me. Our bond had grown through hardships and animosity, and our farewell marked a testament to the camaraderie we had developed. Now, as a fifth termer, it was time for me to reign as a KING!

gate 5:
rise of the kings!

16

The Taste Of Power!

Saurabh, barged into my cabin, fuming with anger.

"I can't believe that, SCC has grounded me and given me cabin number 1. I'm a fifth-termer, and I deserve respect. I swear, I'll kill that asshole," Saurabh ranted.

After a much-needed term break, I was eager to jump back into the academy for the first time ever! Despite still recovering from my leg injury, I was feeling much stronger than before. As I stepped foot into the NDA special, I couldn't help but notice a sense of nervousness amongst the juniors. It was as if they had entered a completely new world. Everywhere I turned, I saw the juniors frantically scurrying away from certain areas, while my coursemates were flexing their newfound authority by doling out punishments left and right. I must admit, I found myself intrigued by the spectacle before me. Suddenly, I too longed to experience that same sense of power!

Did you know that fifth-termers are known as Kings in the academy, while sixth-termers are referred to as Lords? As a cadet, I used to wonder why this was the case since kings were supposed to be greater than lords. But when I finally reached my fifth term, everything started to make sense.

Being a fifth termer was hands down the most lovable experience I had in NDA. We had minimal responsibilities, fewer punishments, and an abundance of free time with endless privileges. I couldn't believe how lucky I was to have reached this stage of my academy journey.

On the other hand, the sixth-termers were always in a frenzy, running the squadron, getting chewed out by the squadron office, and constantly being assigned new tasks.

As the saying goes, karma always comes back to bite you in unexpected ways. Since my first term, I had harbored a strong dislike for two of my immediate seniors. I constantly disobeyed their orders and never gave them any respect. However, when I returned from term break, I was hit with a brutal reality. Both of those seniors had now ascended to the highest positions in the academy. One was the SCC, while the other held the prestigious title of CSM. I knew my life was about to get a lot tougher.

To make matters worse, I was given cabin number 8, which was located directly opposite the CSM's cabin. I felt like my life had taken a turn for the worst, but then something unexpected happened. One of my best friends, Saurabh, barged into my cabin, fuming with anger.

"I can't believe that, SCC has grounded me and given me cabin number 1. I'm a fifth-termer, and I deserve respect. I swear, I'll kill that asshole," Saurabh ranted.

But in the NDA, there's a saying:

"You may feel bad when you're in trouble, but if you look around, you'll see your coursemates are in even deeper trouble, and you'll feel blessed."

It may sound cliché, but it's true. I suddenly realized that I wasn't alone on the ground floor, which was a terrifying place for any cadet. In fact, being on the ground floor came with its own set of benefits that we hadn't considered before.

PROS AND CONS OF GETTING GROUNDED!

	PROS	CONS
1	Faster access to cold coffee and evening snacks: When you're feeling peckish or need a caffeine fix, you don't have to walk far. You can just pop into the central lobby and grab a cold coffee or evening snack.	Cabin cupboard inspections: If you're on the ground floor, your cabin cupboard is more likely to be inspected during inspections
2	Quick escape route: If there is a crossing/officer is on rounds and you're caught in a sticky situation, you can always jump out the window and make a quick escape.	Random cabin checks by officers: As ground floor cabins are easily accessible, any officer can enter your cabin at any time. So, you need to ensure that everything is in order and you're always following the rules.

3.	Join any fall-in in the last 5 seconds: You can easily join any fall-in that's happening on the ground floor at the last second, without worrying about being late or getting punished.	Coursemates asking for things: Being on the ground floor means that you're in a central location and easily accessible to your coursemates. This can be both good and bad. On the one hand, you can socialize more easily with your peers. On the other hand, you might get interrupted by coursemates asking for things like biscuits, pens, or other items.
4.	Best for bunking classes/Locked in Cabin (LIC): If you're planning to skip a class or get LIC, being on the ground floor gives you an added advantage.	
5.	Orderlies always available: Need your laundry done or your cabin cleaned? No problem. Orderlies are always available on the ground floor to help you out with any task.	

PARA SF OFFICERS ARE CRAZY!

The fifth term at NDA was an absolute blast! It was a time of freedom and fun, and I have some of my fondest memories from that term. Walking was no longer a punishable offence, and we could easily sneak off to the Golf Juice Bar or Gole Market on Sundays without any consequences. Plus, we were given more liberty than ever before. It was truly heaven on earth!

This was also the time when the cadets were divided into different classes according to their respective services. Army cadets had the opportunity to experience the rigorous training module of the ATT (Army Training Team), while Naval and Air Force cadets enjoyed their time in the NTT (Naval Cadet Team) and AFTT (Air Force Training Team), respectively. As army cadets, we were fondly referred to as PONGOs, - Permanently On Ground Duty Only. However, our training was intensified beyond belief.

One particular memory that stands out is the day we had a class on **camouflage and concealment**. I was expecting a typical lecture, where we would be taught about different types of camouflage on a blackboard. But, to my surprise, the class was taken by a Para SF officer who barked at us as soon as he saw us:

"Why aren't you guys camouflaged?"

Like everyone else, I had applied olive green camouflage paint to my face and hands. But the officer wasn't satisfied and shouted at us,

"I will give you 10 seconds. I want you all to be properly camouflaged, you fuckers!"

In a frenzy, all of us fifth-termers ran for our lives and quickly repainted our faces. After the ten seconds were up, the officer yelled,

"You cunts have the audacity to defy my orders! I wanted you to go invisible, but are you invisible? No! I will teach you what camouflage and concealment really mean."

For the next seven hours, we were subjected to all sorts of new punishments we had never even heard of in the previous four terms. We rolled around in drains, mud, and whatnot until our bodies and souls were broken. By the time we were finished, our clothes were torn, and we stank of drain water.

"See, that's how you go invisible," the officer said. "I hope you've learned the topic of camouflage and concealment in detail now."

We limped back to our squadron, where our naval and air force counterparts were waiting for us. Avi, an air force cadet, made a mockery of us, saying,

"See these army cadets; that's how you become one with mother earth. Hats off to your love for this soil. I hope there isn't any soil in your asses."

After a humiliating encounter with Avi, I decided to wash away my sorrows with a refreshing bath and fresh clothes. Just as I was about to gear up for my evening games, Sharma came running up to me with excitement written all over his face.

"Brother, are you ready for tonight?" he exclaimed.

I couldn't help but feel puzzled at his sudden burst of energy. "What's happening tonight?" I asked.

"It's a once-in-a-lifetime event, something you won't want to miss," he said with a mischievous grin.

Curiosity piqued, I couldn't resist asking him for more details. "What is it?" I pressed.

"It's the night that only comes around once every four years!" he exclaimed, practically bouncing with excitement.

My mind raced as I tried to figure out what he could possibly be talking about. And then it hit me. Without a second thought, I grabbed my hockey stick and a blanket to celebrate this special occasion in style.

17

A Birthday, A Broken Nose And A Feud!

Panicking, we rushed him to the MH, where the doctor diagnosed a broken nose. The second-termer, who was clearly in agony, managed to come up with a cover story about tripping and falling on his face, sparing us the severe repercussions of our actions. We were relieved, but not for long.

Birthdays at NDA are nothing short of extraordinary. The entire academy is filled with midterm cheer, and on your birthday, you are untouchable - no punishments allowed! As a junior, you eagerly await your birthday, as it's the one day where you can finally catch up on some much-needed sleep. NDA has a unique tradition when it comes to birthdays - a cadet must provide Samosas and Jalebis for the entire squadron and throw a party for his coursemates.

I've always had a soft spot for birthdays, but there was one particular cadet who was always a bit of a spoilsport—Rishi. Rishi's birthday fell on February 29th, and every year on the 28th, he'd shoo us away, insisting that he'd only celebrate on the actual day. It was frustrating, but we had to respect his logic.

Finally, the day we had all been waiting for arrived—Rishi's birthday! And not just any birthday, but his first one in two years, now that we were all fifth-termers. We were determined to make it a celebration to remember.

I can still recall the night vividly: we snuck into Rishi's cabin armed with blankets and hockey sticks, ready to give him a proper birthday thrashing. But as we knocked on the door, something felt off. When Rishi finally opened the door, we threw the blanket over him, and everyone else started beating the blanket with their hockey sticks. But suddenly, Harry sensed something was amiss.

"This doesn't sound like Rishi," Harry said, a note of fear creeping into his voice.

We all froze for a moment, then lifted the blanket to reveal a second-termer hiding beneath it.

Rishi emerged from his cabin, confusion etched on his face.

"I had called this second-termer in for additional punishments for sleeping during the study period," he explained. "It seems you guys have taken care of it for me."

It was only then that we realized what we had done. We had mistakenly thought the second-termer was Rishi and subjected him to a merciless beating. When we finally let him up, blood was gushing from his nose like a river.

Panicking, we rushed him to the MH, where the doctor diagnosed a broken nose. The second-termer, who was clearly in agony, managed to come up with a cover story about tripping and falling on his face, sparing us the severe repercussions of our actions. We were relieved, but not for long.

As we returned to our dorm, we were met by a group of sixth termers who had caught wind of our misdeed. Harry, usually so calm and collected, cursed vehemently for the first time in his life. We knew that the punishment for manhandling a junior was severe - we could lose our term badges and suffer the consequences for the rest of our time at NDA.

Sure enough, our powers as fifth-termers were stripped away, and we were subjected to grueling punishments for the next two weeks. We took our lumps without complaint, knowing that we had brought this upon ourselves. And worst of all, Rishi once again managed to evade throwing a birthday party.

As the days passed, the end of term was fast approaching, and our powers and influence as fifth-termers were growing day by day. One day, as I was on my way to my academic classes, I heard someone bark at me from behind.

"Why in hell are you walking?" the Academy Cadet Captain (ACC) bellowed.

"Sir, I am having some trouble with my leg," I replied, trying to keep my composure.

"Have you passed all your tests?" he asked, looking me over.

"Yes, sir. "In the first attempt," I said proudly.

"Did you run cross country for the squadron?" he asked in a measured tone.

"Yes, sir. Of course," I answered.

"Then why in hell are you walking?" ACC barked with anger.

I realized the trap he had set for me and felt like a rat caught in a trap. Before I could say anything, he ordered me to report to him at 2330H and marched off to his class. My ego was hurt, but with only a few weeks left until he passed out and I became a sixth-termer, I decided not to report to him.

At 2330H that night, I was sleeping peacefully in my cabin when a loud bang on the door startled me. At first, I thought it was one of my coursemates and ignored it. Then came a loud kick on the door, and the latch broke open, revealing ACC standing in front of me. It was the second time in my life that I felt like I might die that night, the first being my first night with my overstudy!

"Sir, I hope I didn't disturb your sleep," ACC said in a voice filled with anger.

"Sir, I had some medicine and then went to sleep," I tried to explain, hoping for some mercy.

He then took me to his squadron and made me stand there for the whole night without any punishment. He simply marked a small box on the ground with white chalk and told me to stay inside it. Initially, it looked easy, but soon it became unbearable. He left me in the morning for classes and ordered me to report again the next night. This continued for twelve days!

On the thirteenth night, the barrier of my patience broke, and I couldn't take it anymore.

"What the hell do you think of yourself when I have clearly told you that I have a problem with my leg, and still, you're making me stand the whole night," I snapped.

Without a word, ACC went inside his cabin and brought out a study chair, placing it inside a bigger box that covered the area occupied by the chair.

"Sit on this chair, but if you fall asleep, you will stand in that small box again," he said patiently.

For the next few hours, the chair felt comfortable, but I eventually dozed off. Whenever I slept, ACC was there to wake me up. This went on for another three nights!

On one night, when my ego was finally crushed, and I saw no way out of this mental torture, I knocked on ACC's cabin.

"What is it?" "Do you want a bed or what?" he shouted from inside.

"Sir, I'm sorry," I said in a low voice.

"Sorry! Sorry for what?" he said as he opened the door.

"Sir, I apologize for showing attitude," I said, trying to sound humble.

ACC brought another chair from his room and sat besides me.

"Only two weeks left!" My ACC, the academy's grooming officer, leant in, his eyes intense. "I am responsible for ensuring every junior is well-prepared before I pass out. And that includes turning you into a good sixth-termer before you leave."

I hung my head, ashamed.

"Sir, I was blinded by power. I lost my way. But I assure you, it won't happen again."

He beckoned me into his cabin, and I followed him inside. As he poured me a cup of cold coffee, I noticed a whiteboard hanging on the wall, filled with his life goals. Becoming an ACC was one thing, but becoming a General was another. I couldn't help but wonder how heavy a burden he carried on his shoulders.

For the next hour, we talked about everything, from our experiences at the academy to our dreams for the future. As he walked me out, I knew that I had learned a valuable lesson from him.

The days that followed were filled with end-of-term activities and POP practice. And then, finally, the day came. My ACC was giving the commands to all contingents on his POP. As soon as it was over, I rushed to his squadron to thank him and say goodbye.

"Thank you, sir," I said, hugging him tightly. "We'll meet again soon."

He chuckled. "Definitely. After all, you're the one who kept me awake for two weeks straight!"

I returned to my squadron, said my goodbyes to seniors, and packed my bags. With only one gate left to pass out from this academy, I felt a mix of pride and sadness. But as I boarded the NDA Special and returned home as a sixth-termer, I knew I had grown in ways I never thought possible. And I had my ACC to thank for it.

gate 6:
reign of the lords!

18

My NDA Ball!

The day before the ball, I collected the ball passes and called my partner,

"Where am I supposed to meet you?" I have to give you the passes."

"Passes are not required," she said confidently.

As I packed my bags for my last term at NDA, I couldn't help but remember the look on my parents' faces. As a cadet, NDA was tough, but for my parents, it was even tougher. They worried about me constantly, even when I was happy. I still remember how I would waste half of my free time on Sundays standing in line for a telephone call in the Gole Market. Sometimes, I would even give my father's mobile number to the person on the phone and ask him to call my parents to let them know that I was okay!

I'll never forget the day I went home with a broken knee. I hadn't told my parents about the injury, and when I arrived home, my mother couldn't stop crying for days. She tried everything, applying all sorts of ointments she found on

YouTube to my knee and asking me how I felt. I would just give her a fake smile and say,

Wow, Maa, it has reduced the pain so much; I think I can run now."

But now, as a sixth-termer, everything was different. There was no one to punish me or tell me to do PT or go to games. I had all the privileges I once desired, including the luxury of sleeping in until 15 minutes before ODT. But with those privileges came a heavy responsibility. As a sixth-termer, I had to perform better than the juniors, get to the fields for games before them, and do everything in the best way possible.

Despite the challenges, I was able to sail through my tests and cross country without any difficulty. But as an army cadet, our sixth term was full of long classes full of ragda. I still remember our firing classes, where we had seven hours to fire just five bullets. And out of those seven hours, six hours and fifty-nine minutes were spent on various punishments.

But our basic events were soon over, and we were introduced to Camp Torna!

CAMP TORNA

Camp Torna is one of the toughest training camps in the NDA, designed to provide rigors physical and mental training to the cadets preparing to become officers in the Indian Armed Forces. I still remember the first time I heard about Torna—I was intimidated yet excited to experience what it had in store for me.

During the camp, we underwent various types of training, including rock climbing, trekking, obstacle courses, and other outdoor activities designed to test our endurance, leadership skills, and teamwork. Torna was a unique camp—the distances of the josh run increased up to 60 kilometers, and the ragda multiplied manifold times. Torna, a Hindi word meaning "to break," was a camp that truly broke my body and mind, but not my coursemate spirit and camaraderie. For all of us, it was comparatively easier than the Rovers camp because we had grown physically and mentally.

After completing the Rovers' josh run and landing in our squadron, we started preparing for the next big event—the NDA Ball.

NDA BALL

Every NDA cadet dreams of attending this great event. As a junior, we were never allowed to witness the NDA Ball in person, so our excitement was on the seventh heaven. It was a privilege meant for only sixth-termers. As a junior, we were sent to Habibulla Hall several hours prior to the NDA Ball and left after it was over. In Habibulla Hall, we were shown the worst movies possible, and our dinner used to be in Habibulla Hall itself. So as juniors, we never got to see any beautiful girls on campus.

The most challenging part of the NDA Ball was finding a ball partner. As sixth-termers, we were given liberties every Sunday. Some of us had been successful in making a girlfriend since the last five terms, whereas for most of us, it had to be done in the sixth term. Every Sunday, our routine was simple. We caught a bus to the city, had a Daveli (a local dish in Pune) and Cad B (chocolate shake), and then started our mission to get a ball partner.

I had developed confidence in approaching girls over the last few terms. I remember the time when I was eating a Daveli, and I saw a girl across the street in a café reading a book and having her coffee. Like always, I fell in love with her the very next second. But since my experience of approaching Rhea didn't go well, I decided to maintain my posture. I approached her and very confidently said, "Hi."

"Hi Cadet," she replied.

I was about to invite her to the ball party when she said, "And yes, I know about your ball party. I am busy on that date, but since you are the guy who has approached me so confidently, I will try my best."

Then we sat down for 15 minutes, had a cup of coffee, and when I was about to leave, she called me and said,

"Cadet, how am I supposed to contact you?"

I was so happy that I had completely forgotten to take her number. Then we exchanged mobile phones. I still remember writing her number on my hand with a ballpoint pen refill. While going back to the academy, I had seen that number so many times that it was clearly etched in my mind now. Also, like any typical love-struck cadet, I didn't wash that hand for the whole day. I then reached my cabin and saved her number on my mobile phone!

As a cadet at the academy, I knew the rules stated that mobile phones were not allowed, but like any typical cadet, I took a risk and hid it in my cabin. Sometimes I would even put it in a shoe or inside a book. But as a good junior, if you land in NDA, you shouldn't keep a phone as it could make you lose a term!

That night, I had a little chat with her on my phone and convinced her to come to my ball party. I was super excited and couldn't sleep the whole night. My intention wasn't to make her my girlfriend, but to prove to my juniors that I could get a partner for my Ball night.

The news of me getting a ball partner spread like wildfire, and soon, my beggar coursemates were offering me their juice and biscuits, begging me to manage their ball partners too. I asked my ball partner to ask her friends to accompany her to Ball, and she agreed. The night before the ball, she confirmed that she was coming to Ball with her six friends. My coursemates hugged me and thanked me for that favor.

The day before the ball, I collected the ball passes and called my partner,

"Where am I supposed to meet you?" I have to give you the passes."

"Passes are not required," she said confidently.

I tried to make her understand that passes were necessary to enter NDA, but she replied,

"Ok, if you insist, I am sitting here in Gole Market. You can give me the passes here."

Her words sent shivers down my spine, and I ran towards the Gole market at full speed, where she was eating ice cream.

"What are you doing here?" I asked, catching my breath.

"I live here in NDA," she replied, still eating her ice cream.

We sat down for a few minutes to clear up the confusion. She told me that her father was the Battalion commander of the

Abhimanyu Battalion. At first, I was depressed about this new information, but she assured me that she had informed her dad about the ball and hadn't told anyone about my phone. At that moment, I had mad respect for her!

The night of the ball had finally arrived, and the excitement in the air was palpable. The cadets were dressed in their best uniforms, and the ball partners looked absolutely stunning in their gowns. As the couples marched off to the mess, the band began playing a lively tune, setting the mood for the evening.

Upon entering the mess, the cadets and their partners were greeted by the grandeur of the hall, which had been decorated with colorful lights and flowers. The tables were set with fine china and silverware, and the aroma of delicious food filled the air.

As the music started, the couples took to the dance floor, twirling and swaying to the rhythm of the music. The ballroom was alive with energy and excitement as the couples danced the night away.

We, too, were showing off our dance moves, and all the cadets and their partners were beaming with joy as they twirled around the dance floor. The music was enchanting, and the atmosphere was electric.

The dinner served during the ball was nothing short of exquisite. The chefs had prepared a sumptuous feast of delectable dishes, and the guests savored every bite.

As the night wore on, we continued to dance, talk, and enjoy each other's company. It was a magical evening that they would remember for years to come.

The ball night had been a dream come true, filled with laughter, love, and joy. And as we bid each other farewell, we knew that this was a night we would cherish forever.

19

My NDA POP!

The Passing Out Parade (POP) at the National Defence Academy holds a special place in every cadet's heart. It marks the end of three grueling years of training, and the "ragda" that kept us awake for countless nights gets finally over.

I started this journey with my coursemates, a band of brothers with whom I shared my struggles, my joys, and my fears. Some of us were relegated, many were injured, but we were among the fortunate ones who made it to the end. The POP practices were hectic and tiring, and I, like every other cadet, was eagerly waiting for the day when they would finally be over.

The hard work that a cadet puts in for the POP cannot be described in words. We had already handed over our powers to the fifth-termers, and with only one week left until POP, we were getting ready for our last practice. I still vividly recall a first-termer yelling at me during Grudges Day, and it reminded me of my own early days when I was in his shoes.

The academy allowed our parents to visit three days before the POP. They were accommodated and provided with the best food and facilities. Our juniors gave them a tour of NDA, showing them various events from horseback riding to khukuri dance and Judo. This event was called "NDA

Darshan," and it was a special time for us to bond with our families.

On the day of the POP, the cadets were standing in the quartermaster fort, preparing for their last practice, while our parents sat in the audience, eagerly waiting for the parade to begin. The Academy Cadet Captain (ACC), who was considered a terror for the juniors, came forwards and motivated us for the last parade. His voice was emotional and breaking, but he managed to ask us one last time,

"Will you give your best for me today?"

All the cadets shouted back in unison, " Yes, sir!" and their voices echoed across the parade ground, energizing the audience.

Then, it was the turn of our drill ustaad, the same person who was once our arch-enemy. He came forwards and spoke with emotion in his voice,

"Next time we meet, you'll all be officers. Don't forget about me. Will you show me your best drill today for the last time?"

All the cadets responded with a resounding "Yes, ustaad!" sending a wave of energy to the audience.

Finally, the Adjutant arrived on his white horse. He was always strict, but he cracked a joke on this day and said,

"From today onwards, you are my brother officers. Keep doing well in life."

The beagle was blown, signaling the start of the POP. The drums began to beat, and the energy of the sixth-termers reached seventh heaven! Tears and emotions ran high as all the cadets got fired up to perform the best drill practice of their lives.

The gates of the quartermaster's fort opened, and all contingents began marching towards the parade ground, their movements and hearts synchronizing as they marched out gracefully. This was the day we had all been waiting for, and it was a moment that we would cherish forever.

As the contingents came to a halt, a loud stamping of feet sent shockwaves through the audience, leaving them in awe of the beauty of the moment. Among the onlookers were my parents, who had suffered the most during my training, always worried about my health and well-being. Despite everyone holding a phone in their hands, they searched through the contingents to find their son among the many faces.

My father, now a respected figure who had always instructed me to face tough times with a smile, was trying to control his tears. As he clapped, the worst days of his life flashed before his eyes, and he cried like a baby. My mother, who had always prayed for my health, was now the strongest lady on earth, shouting at the top of her voice and pointing at my father, See, that's our Golu; he's right there! Can you see him?"

And then there was me - Golu, standing in the first line, looking for my parents among the audience. I had waited for this day to come, but I didn't want to leave the academy. The emotional weight of the moment was almost unbearable. I thought about my coursemates, who had become like family to me over the past three years, and how I wouldn't be able to see them again, especially the Air Force and Naval Cadets who wouldn't accompany me to the next training academy. I thought about the juniors who had disturbed me on Sunday mornings for game practices and realized that I would miss them too.

As the drums beat and everyone marched, I was lost in my own world, and every word of command caused me to hit the butt of my rifle so hard that blood started to ooze out of my fingers. But I didn't feel any pain; I was too emotional to care. The three years that seemed like a century flashed before my eyes in mere seconds.

Then, I saw my parents waving at me like small children, and I couldn't maintain my military posture any longer. Tears rolled down my cheeks as I charged towards them, stamping my feet even harder. The slow march began, and we marched towards the "Antim Pag," the last stair crossing that would complete our tenure in the academy. With each step, my breath got heavier, and I couldn't believe that my dream was becoming a reality.

Finally, I reached the last step and stamped on it with all my might, wanting to break it once and for all. But the "Antim Pag" had faced many such cadets and many such stamps since time immemorial and didn't break.

We rushed to the Manoj Pandey Block, opposite the parade ground, where our Squadron Commander and other officers were waiting for us. They congratulated us on our success and hugged us. I did squadron push-ups with my coursemates, danced, and enjoyed the moment, which was only mine.

After the celebration, I returned to the squadron, where juniors were waiting for me to give them sweets. I spent some time with them and then marched off to my room, where

Dabral was waiting for me with tears in his eyes. I was reminded of the time when I was in his place a year ago.

"How will I survive in this academy without you, sir?" asked Dabral.

"You will, Dabral, you will," I said confidently. "Now you are a fifth-termer with a lot of responsibilities. Just keep working hard."

"I will, sir, I will," said Dabral with a spark in his eyes.

As I packed my bags and walked towards my car, my heart felt heavy with emotion. I couldn't believe that my time at the squadron had come to an end. I turned back for one last look at the place that had been my home for the past few years. The memories flooded my mind and brought tears to my eyes.

I remembered the tough training, the early morning drills, and the long hours of studying. But I also remembered the moments of camaraderie and brotherhood that we shared. The times when we laughed together, supported each other, and celebrated our victories.

As I sat in the car with my parents, I couldn't help but feel grateful for everything that the squadron had given me. It was more than just a training ground; it was a place where I had grown into a man, thanks to the guidance and support of my mentors and coursemates.

With a renewed sense of purpose, I looked toward the future. The Indian Military Academy awaited me, and I was determined to make my squadron proud. I vowed to carry the lessons and values I had learned at the NDA throughout my life.

As we drove away from the squadron, I felt a mix of sadness and excitement. The memories would always stay with me, but I was ready for the next chapter of my life. I was now an **'Ex NDA'**, a proud cadet who had completed his training with honor and dignity. And I knew that whatever challenges lay ahead, I would face them with the courage and resilience that I had learned at the NDA.

Epilogue

As the sun set over the picturesque city of Dehradun, we stood at attention on the parade ground of the Indian Military Academy. My coursemates and I had completed our training at the National Defence Academy and had now arrived at the IMA to continue our journey as army officers.

The Adjutant of the academy, a stern-looking Lieutenant Colonel, walked up to us and inspected us with a critical eye. He then stepped forward and addressed us.

"Gentlemen, welcome to the Indian Military Academy. You have already proven yourselves as capable and disciplined soldiers during your time at the NDA, and we expect nothing less from you here. The training here will be intense, but I assure you, it will prepare you for the challenges that lie ahead."

As the colonel walked away, my thoughts drifted back to the memories of my time at the NDA. The grueling physical training, the rigorous academic curriculum, and the unforgettable camaraderie with my coursemates - all of it had prepared me for this moment. I knew that the journey ahead would be tough, but I was ready to face it head-on.

My coursemates and I exchanged glances, each of us silently acknowledging our unspoken bond. We had come a long way from the day we first set foot in the NDA, and we knew we had a long way to go. But we were ready - ready to serve our country with honor, courage, and pride.

As we marched toward our companies, I felt a sense of excitement and anticipation wash over me. The journey ahead would be challenging, but it would also be rewarding. I was ready to take on whatever lay ahead and knew that my coursemates felt the same.

We had graduated from the NDA as brothers-in-arms, and we would continue to serve together as brothers-in-arms at the IMA and beyond. Our journey had just begun, and I was eager to see where it would take us next.

Mission 100

As an Indian Army officer, I am always looking for ways to make a positive impact on the world around me. That's why I have decided to embark on a new challenge called "Mission 100". The goal of this mission is to educate 100 children from the remotest corners of India and to empower them to contribute positively to society.

Although I have not yet started on this mission, I have begun working on generating the necessary resources to make it a reality. I have started a YouTube channel and have decided to adopt all legal and ethical ways to generate enough revenue including writing books on various topics related to education and empowerment.

Through my YouTube channel and Instagram page, I aim to inspire and educate people about the importance of education and the impact it can have on individuals and society. I share stories of individuals who have overcome challenges to achieve success and inspire others to do the same. I also provide practical tips and advice on how to improve one's life through education and personal development.

I am passionate about the potential of education to transform lives, and I believe that every child deserves access to quality education. Through Mission 100, I hope to provide children from some of the most disadvantaged communities in India with the education they need to succeed.

I know that this mission will not be easy, and it will require a lot of effort and resources. However, I am committed to seeing it through. I believe that with hard work and determination, I can make a real difference in the lives of these children and empower them to achieve their full potential.

Through my YouTube channel and books, I hope to inspire others to join me in this mission. Whether it's through donating time or resources, or simply spreading the word, every contribution counts. Together, we can make a difference and create a brighter future for India.

WHAT KEEPS ME GOING!

> Sir just got recommended for NDA. Will be joining NDA. All because of you sir. Will train hard and join your Paltan 😊

> Sir please ye YT channel band mat krna. Sir hum yha NDA mai aapke meme chup chupke dekhte hai aur haste hai.. yha aapka hi naara hai.. Sir bas chahe kitna bhi kaam bad jae fauj ka - apne chote bhaiyo behno ke lie time nikaal lena ✅ 🙏

> Hey sir, I remember the time i was getting suicidal feelings after geting rejected each time in SSB. You were the one who reached out to me in my toughest times and that one audio calp of 8 minutes changed my life. I am going to NDA sir and will definitely join your paltan. Sir you are god for me.

> Sir mai yha SSB allahabad aaya tha aur recommend ho gya.. sir sab log aapko jaante hai.. aapki hi baatein chalti haii yha. Sir aap great ho!

> Jai Hind sir
> Sir got recommended for TES. I did what you said - everything the exact way. Sir lots of love to you. Aapka ye chota bhai aapko kabi ni bhulega.

> Hii sir
> Going to MNS. Your memes and your channel was a dose which kept me going. Sir mai commission hoke aapko pakka milungi. Take care sir

> Sir mai yha SSB allahabad aaya tha aur recommend ho gya.. sir sab log aapko jaante hai.. aapki hi baatein chalti haii yha. Sir aap great ho!

> Sir you are the best YouTuber out there. Lots of love 😊

> Sir yad hai aapko jab pichli bar mai conference out hua tha aur bohttt dukhi thaa
> Sir aapko yad ni hoga but aapne ek baat boli thi
>
> You aren't a looser if you fight and loose but you are the biggest looser if you quit without fighting.
>
> Sir is baar recommend ho gya. Sir aapki baatein jaadu haii - Magic. Sir mai Jaipur se hu- kabhi aao toh btana - banda aapke lie jaan bhi de dega...

> Hellllooooo sirrrrr, CDS ho gyaa.. Aapko aur momo bhabhi ko boht boht boht boht pyaar. Comission hoke aapke jesa banna hai aur aapko milna hai.
>
> I know aapko shayd ye message dekhne ka time na mile sir. Par aapki ek video ne mera army join krne ka man bna dia. And when i watched more of your videos, i decided to become like you. Sir i going to IMA and will passout in 18 months. Sir bas ek wish hai ki aapse milu. Aap mere bhai ho. Apko ek bar gale lagana hai. Sir i love you. Milte hai sir jaldi hi.

> Sir sir sir!!!!!!!
>
> Sir aapne ek mera qna mai question answer kia tha and guess what interviewing officer ne wo pooch lia. Sir maine same jawab dia bindaaas hoke, tension free hoke.
>
> Sir officer ne poocha ki aap kya coaching leke aaye ho, maine boht proudly aapka naam lia aur btaya ki aapse seekha hai. Sir mai merit in ho gya hu aur CTW ja rha hu.
>
> Sir commission hote hi aapko milungaaa aur party kreinge 😊 😊😊

www.ingramcontent.com/pod-product-compliance
Lightning Source LLC
LaVergne TN
LVHW061614070526
838199LV00078B/7283